ON THE STREET WHERE YOU LIVE

"Is a reincarnated serial killer at work in a New Jersey resort town more than a century after he first drew blood? That's the catchy premise that supports Clark's 24th book. . . . [A] plot-driven novel."
— *Publishers Weekly*

"As the bodies pile up—and the suspect list grows—her chatty style and plot surprises make a reader want to settle in."
— *People magazine*

BEFORE I SAY GOOD-BYE

"Mary Higgins Clark knows what she's doing. . . . This savvy author always comes up with something unexpected. . . . A hold-your-breath ending."
— *The New York Times Book Review*

"Romantic suspense has no more reliable champion than Mary Higgins Clark. Her characters are . . . breezy and fun, and so is this confection of a book."
— *Publishers Weekly*

ALSO BY MARY HIGGINS CLARK

MARY
HIGGINS
CLARK

Where Are the Children?

Simon & Schuster Paperbacks

NEW YORK LONDON TORONTO SYDNEY NEW DELHI

Simon & Schuster Paperbacks
An Imprint of Simon & Schuster, Inc.
1230 Avenue of the Americas
New York, NY 10020

This Simon & Schuster trade paperback edition May 2023

SIMON & SCHUSTER PAPERBACKS and colophon are registered trademarks of Simon & Schuster, Inc.

For information about special discounts for bulk purchases, please contact Simon & Schuster Special Sales at 1-866-506-1949 or business@simonandschuster.com.

The Simon & Schuster Speakers Bureau can bring authors to your live event. For more information or to book an event, contact the Simon & Schuster Speakers Bureau at 1-866-248-3049 or visit our website at www.simonspeakers.com.

Manufactured in the United States of America

1 3 5 7 9 10 8 6 4 2

Library of Congress Cataloging-in-Publication Data has been applied for.

ISBN 978-1-6680-2181-1
ISBN 978-0-7432-0611-2 (ebook)

To the memory of my mother,

Nora C. Higgins,

with love, admiration, and gratitude

Where Are the Children?:
An Appreciation

My memory of reading *Where Are the Children?* has always been extremely specific and full of sensory details: *My family is in Maine for a long vacation, five weeks on a tiny point of land that juts into the Casco Bay. There are rickety wooden staircases leading down to the rocky beaches and when the tide comes in at sunset, it crashes against the rocks in dramatic fashion. The cottage has a tin roof and during the summer thunderstorms that sweep through, it is immensely satisfying to curl up under a quilt and read while the rain thrums on the roof. And what could be better company than this grown-up book, filched from my mother or sister, the most shocking, suspenseful, dramatic story I've ever read?*

The only problem with the memory described above is that it's totally false. That Maine vacation happened in 1970, five years before *Where Are the Children?* was published. Why have I relocated the memory to the wrong time and place? I think it's because Mary Higgins Clark's vividly rendered depiction of windswept Cape Cod made me feel as if I lived in that book, that I was one of the children who went missing, yet also their frantic but brave mother, their resolute father. I was everyone but the villain.

It's hard to overstate how transformative *Where Are the Children?* was for a generation of readers, some of whom would grow up to be writers in the very field that Mary essentially created:

domestic suspense. Her use of short chapters, a commonplace technique now, was extremely innovative at the time. Perhaps forty years from now, another crime writer will pen a love letter to *Gone Girl*, a similarly seminal book. Hey, if I'm still around, I'll happily do it. But right now, it's Mary's turn.

Like many novelists before and since, Mary was inspired by a real-life case, the trial of Alice Crimmins, charged with murdering her young son and daughter. In the pre-CNN world of the 1960s, the case didn't become a national sensation, but it received obsessive coverage in the New York metropolitan area, inspiring intense arguments as to Crimmins's guilt or innocence. And while she was found guilty, those convictions were overturned. Released from prison, Crimmins relocated and changed her name. But Mary did what all novelists do, what she had, in fact, been taught in a writing class: She began asking herself a series of "What if?" and "Suppose . . . ?"questions, speculating on what might happen if such a woman had a chance to start a new life. She chose Cape Cod as her setting because she had recently started renting a summer cottage there.

Where Are the Children? was Mary's first suspense novel—she had published a historical novel based on the life of George Washington in 1968—but all the hallmarks of her work are here: a strong, resourceful female protagonist in Nancy Harmon; a vivid setting; a twisting, propulsive storyline that surprises while always playing fair with the reader. Most important, Mary's work has something that cannot be taught or faked: Her books are page-turners, unputdownable.

You may notice that I call her "Mary." I had the good fortune to meet her several times and it was always a joy. She was a gracious, generous presence in the world of crime writers, appearing at conferences and banquets in gorgeous clothes and stunning jewelry, hair in an elegant updo. I remember her sweeping into a hotel bar where several writers had gathered at day's end, stamping her perfectly shod foot in mock indignation that we had been socializing while she had just finished yet another book signing: "You young women have so much fun now."

Mary's teasing was rooted in something profound: It's lonely, being an outlier. Mary preceded—created, in part—an earnest change in the world of crime writing, which wasn't exactly robust in the mid-1970s. By the 1980s, female PI writers Sue Grafton, Marcia Mueller, and Sara Paretsky would breathe new life into that subgenre; the 1990s brought some of the superstars still working today, including Michael Connelly, Harlan Coben, and Lee Child. Popular romance writers such as Tess Gerritsen segued to suspense and saw their audiences increase exponentially. Could it have happened without Mary? Possibly, but it doesn't seem hyperbolic to offer her partial credit.

Mary Higgins Clark would have been a great Mary Higgins Clark character. Born in 1927 to John and Nora Higgins, she began writing at age six. In 1939, her father died, creating multiple hardships for Nora Higgins and her three children. Mary worked as a flight attendant, but she never gave up on her true passion, writing. She took classes when she could and even published a short story inspired by her experiences as a flight attendant.

Flash forward twenty-five years: Mary, who had married Warren Clark in 1949 and had five children, was widowed when her husband died of a heart attack. She supported her family through her writing—radio scripts, short stories.

When the George Washington novel fell short of financial success, Mary decided to study her own bookshelves to figure out how to write a novel that will reach a wide audience. She realized that she had always been a mystery fan, moving from the girl detectives Judy Bolton and Nancy Drew to Golden Age writers such as Agatha Christie, Josephine Tey, and Ngaio Marsh.

Mary quickly saw how much she had intuited about storytelling from these books she loves. In her foreword to the thirtieth anniversary edition of *Where Are the Children?*, she describes her approach to suspense as a system of stones and breadcrumbs, similar to the items Hansel and Gretel used to mark their paths in and out of the woods. "The breadcrumbs, so quickly gobbled up, turn out to not to be the clues they seemed, while the stones, which blend in so well with the landscape, often prove to be the true guide to finding the solution to the crime." In other words, it's not enough to have red herrings, which draw the eye, although we may wish to gobble them up. The integrity of a suspense novel depends on the real clues that were always there, but artfully hidden.

To achieve this, a writer must never condescend to the readers. Mary held her readers in high regard; it is impossible to imagine her ignoring continuity errors, as Harold Robbins is said to have done, with the airy dismissal that his fans wouldn't notice. And even as the world coarsened, Mary held true to her own values, disdaining explicit language and sex, while still managing to write delightful romantic subplots.

Of all the details in Mary's account of writing and publishing *Where Are the Children?*, two stand out to me. One, she remembers exactly what she was wearing when she delivered the book to her agent's secretary: a black-and-white suit. Better still, she wrote in her journal, "I have finished the book and it is GOOD!!!"

Her agent agreed, as did the legendary editor Phyllis Grann, an editor at Simon & Schuster at the time. So did millions and millions of readers, including me, even if I can't tell you where I was when I read it, or how old I was. (Not in Maine, however, and not eleven years old; we can be sure of that much.) Mary Higgins Clark wrote a book, changed her life, and changed publishing while she was at it. She may not have realized how monumental her achievement was the day she delivered her manuscript, but I wish for all writers, everywhere, a moment when you look at your pages and say to yourself, as Mary did, "I have finished the book and it is GOOD!!!"

Laura Lippman
Baltimore, Maryland
December 2022

Prologue

He could feel the chill coming in through the cracks around the windowpanes. Clumsily he got up and lumbered over to the window. Reaching for one of the thick towels he kept handy, he stuffed it around the rotting frame.

The incoming draft made a soft, hissing sound in the towel, a sound that vaguely pleased him. He looked out at the mist-filled sky and studied the whitecaps churning in the water. From this side of the house it was often possible to see Province-town, on the opposite shore of Cape Cod Bay.

He hated the Cape. He hated the bleakness of it on a November day like this; the stark grayness of the water; the stolid people who didn't say much but studied you with their eyes. He had hated it the one summer he'd been here—waves of tourists sprawling on the beaches; climbing up the steep embankment to this house; gawking in the downstairs windows, cupping their hands over their eyes to peer inside.

He hated the large FOR SALE sign that Ray Eldredge had posted on the front and back of the big house and the fact that now Ray and that woman who worked for him had begun bringing people in to see the house. Last month it had been only a matter of luck that he'd come along as they'd started through; only luck that he'd gotten to the top floor before they had and been able to put away the telescope.

Time was running out. Somebody would buy this house and he wouldn't be able to rent it again. That was why he'd sent the article to the paper. He wanted to still be here to enjoy seeing her exposed for what she was in front of these people . . . now, when she must have started to feel safe.

There was something else that he had to do, but the chance had never come. She kept such a close watch on the children. But he couldn't afford to wait anymore. Tomorrow . . .

He moved restlessly around the room. The bedroom of the top-floor apartment was large. The whole house was large. It was a bastardized evolution of an old captain's house. Begun in the seventeenth century on a rocky crest that commanded a view of the whole bay, it was a pretentious monument to man's need to be forever on guard.

Life wasn't like that. It was bits and pieces. Icebergs that showed in tips. He knew. He rubbed his hand over his face, feeling warm and uncomfortable even though the room was chilly. For six years now he'd rented this house in the late summer and fall. It was almost exactly as it had been when he had first come into it. Only a few things were different: the telescope in the front room; the clothes that he kept for the special times; the peaked cap that he pulled over his face, which shaded it so well.

Otherwise the apartment was the same: the old-fashioned sofa and pine tables and hooked rug in the living room; the rock maple bedroom set. This house and apartment had been ideal for his purpose until this fall, when Ray Eldredge had told him they were actively trying to sell the place for a restaurant and it could be rented only with the understanding it could be shown on telephoned notice.

Raynor Eldredge. The thought of the man brought a smile.

What would Ray think tomorrow when he saw the story? Had Nancy ever told Ray who she was? Maybe not. Women could be sly. If Ray didn't know, it would be even better. How wonderful it would be to actually see Ray's expression when he opened the paper! It was delivered a little after ten in the morning. Ray would be in his office. He might not even look at it for a while.

Impatiently, he turned from the window. His thick, trunklike legs were tight in shiny black trousers. He'd be glad when he could lose some of this weight. It would mean that awful business of starving himself again, but he could do it. When it had been necessary he'd done it before. Restlessly he rubbed a hand over his vaguely itchy scalp. He'd be glad when he could let his hair grow back in its natural lines again. The sides had always been thick and would probably be mostly gray now.

He ran one hand slowly down his trouser leg, then impatiently paced around the apartment, finally stopping at the telescope in the living room. The telescope was especially powerful—the kind of equipment that wasn't available for general sale. Even many police departments didn't have it yet. But there were always ways to get things you wanted. He bent over and peered into it, squinting one eye.

Because of the darkness of the day, the kitchen light was on, so it was easy to see Nancy clearly. She was standing in front of the kitchen window, the one that was over the sink. Maybe she was about to get something ready to put into the oven for dinner. But she had a warm jacket on, so she was probably going out. She was standing quietly, just looking in the direction of the water. What was she thinking of? Whom was she thinking of? The children— Peter . . . Lisa . . . ? He'd like to know.

He could feel his mouth go dry and licked his lips nervously. She looked very young today. Her hair was pulled back from her face. She kept it dark brown. Someone would surely have recognized her if she'd left it the natural red-gold shade. Tomorrow she'd be thirty-two. But she still didn't look her age. She had an intriguing young quality, soft and fresh and silky.

He swallowed nervously. He could feel the feverish dryness of his mouth, even while his hands and armpits were wet and warm. He gulped, then swallowed again, and the sound evolved into a deep chuckle. His whole body began to shake with mirth and jarred the telescope. Nancy's image blurred, but he didn't bother refocusing the lens. He wasn't interested in watching her anymore today.

Tomorrow! He could just see the expression she'd have at this time tomorrow. Exposed to the world for what she was; numbed with worry and fear; trying to answer the question . . . the same question the police had thrown at her over and over seven years ago.

"Come on, Nancy," the police would be saying again. "Come clean with us. Tell the truth. You should know you can't get away with this. Tell us, Nancy—where are the children?"

1

Ray came down the stairs pulling the knot closed on his tie. Nancy was sitting at the table with a still-sleepy Missy on her lap. Michael was eating his breakfast in his poised, reflective way.

Ray tousled Mike's head and leaned over to kiss Missy. Nancy smiled up at him. She was so darn pretty. There were fine lines around those blue eyes, but you'd still never take her for thirty-two. Ray was only a few years older himself, but always felt infinitely her senior. Maybe it was that awful vulnerability. He noticed the traces of red at the roots of her dark hair. A dozen times in the last year he'd wanted to ask her to let it grow out, but hadn't dared.

"Happy birthday, honey," he said quietly.

He watched as the color drained from her face.

Michael looked surprised. "Is it Mommy's birthday? You didn't tell me that."

Missy sat upright. "Mommy's birthday?" She sounded pleased.

"Yes," Ray told them. Nancy was staring down at the table. "And tonight we're going to celebrate. Tonight I'm going to bring home a big birthday cake and a present, and we'll have Aunt Dorothy come to dinner. Right, Mommy?"

"Ray . . . no." Nancy's voice was low and pleading.

"Yes. Remember, last year you promised that this year we'd . . ."

Celebrate was the wrong word. He couldn't say it. But for a long time he'd known that they would someday have to start changing the pattern of her birthdays. At first she'd withdrawn completely from him and gone around the house or walked the beach like a silent ghost in a world of her own.

But last year she'd finally begun to talk about them . . . the two other children. She'd said, "They'd be so big now . . . ten and eleven. I try to think how they would look now, but can't seem to even imagine. . . . Everything about that time is so blurred. Like a nightmare that I only dreamed."

"It's supposed to be like that," Ray told her. "Put it all behind you, honey. Don't even wonder what happened anymore."

The memory strengthened his decision. He bent over Nancy and patted her hair with a gesture that was at once protective and gentle.

Nancy looked up at him. The appeal on her face changed to uncertainty. "I don't think—"

Michael interrupted her. "How old are you, Mommy?" he asked practically.

Nancy smiled—a real smile that miraculously eased the tension. "None of your business," she told him.

Ray took a quick gulp of her coffee. "Good girl," he said. "Tell you what, Mike. I'll pick you up after school this afternoon and we'll go get a present for Mommy. Now I'd better get out of here. Some guy is coming up to see the Hunt place. I want to get the file together."

"Isn't it rented?" Nancy asked.

"Yes. That Parrish fellow who's taken the apartment on and off has it again. But he knows we have the right to show it anytime. It's a great spot for a restaurant and wouldn't take much to convert. It'll make a nice commission if I sell it."

Nancy put Missy down and walked with him to the door. He kissed her lightly and felt her lips tremble under his. How much had he upset her by starting this birthday talk? Some instinct made him want to say, *Let's not wait for tonight. I'll stay home and we'll take the kids and go to Boston for the day.*

Instead he got into his car, waved, backed up and drove onto the narrow dirt lane that wound through an acre of woods until it terminated on the cross-Cape road that led to the center of Adams Port and his office.

Ray was right, Nancy thought as she walked slowly back to the table. There was a time to stop following the patterns of yesterday—a time to stop remembering and look only to the future. She knew that a part of her was still frozen. She knew that the mind dropped a protective curtain over painful memories—but it was more than that.

It was as though her life with Carl were a blur . . . the entire time. It was hard to remember the faculty house on the campus, Carl's modulated voice . . . Peter and Lisa. What had they looked like? Dark hair, both of them, like Carl's, and too quiet . . . too subdued . . . affected by her uncertainty . . . and then lost—both of them.

"Mommy, why do you look so sad?" Michael gazed at her with Ray's candid expression, spoke with Ray's directness.

Seven years, Nancy thought. Life was a series of seven-year cycles. Carl used to say that your whole body changed in that time. Every cell renewed itself. It was time for her to really look ahead . . . to forget.

She glanced around the large, cheerful kitchen with the old brick fireplace, the wide oak floors, the red curtains and valances that didn't obstruct the view over the harbor. And then she looked at Michael and Missy. . . .

"I'm not sad, darling," she said. "I'm really not."

She scooped Missy up in her arms, feeling the warmth and sweet stickiness of her. "I've been thinking about your present,"

Missy said. Her long strawberry-blond hair curled around her ears and forehead. People sometimes asked where she got that beautiful hair—who had been the redhead in the family?

"Great," Nancy told her. "But think about it outside. You'd better get some fresh air soon. It's supposed to rain later and get very cold."

After the children were dressed, she helped them on with their windbreakers and hats. "There's my dollar," Michael said with satisfaction as he reached into the breast pocket of his jacket. "I was sure I left it here. Now I can buy you a present."

"Me has money too." Missy proudly held up a handful of pennies. "Oh, now, you two shouldn't be carrying your money out," Nancy told them. "You'll only lose it. Let me hold it for you."

Michael shook his head. "If I give it to you, I might forget it when I go shopping with Daddy."

"I promise I won't let you forget it."

"My pocket has a zipper. See? I'll keep it in that, and I'll hold Missy's for her."

"Well . . ." Nancy shrugged and gave up the discussion. She knew perfectly well that Michael wouldn't lose the dollar. He was like Ray, well organized. "Now, Mike, I'm going to straighten up. You be sure to stay with Missy."

"Okay," Michael said cheerfully. "Come on, Missy. I'll push you on the swing first."

Ray had built a swing for the children. It was suspended from a branch of the massive oak tree at the edge of the woods behind their house.

Nancy pulled Missy's mittens over her hands. They were bright red; fuzzy angora stitching formed a smile face on their backs. "Leave these on," she told her; "otherwise your hands will get cold. It's really getting raw. I'm not even sure you should go out at all."

"Oh, please!" Missy's lip began to quiver.

"All right, all right, don't go into the act," Nancy said hastily. "But not more than half an hour."

She opened the back door and let them out, then shivered as the chilling breeze enveloped her. She closed the door quickly and started up the staircase. The house was an authentic old Cape, and the stairway was almost totally vertical. Ray said that the old settlers must have had a bit of mountain goat in them the way they built their staircases. But Nancy loved everything about this place.

She could still remember the feeling of peace and welcome it had given her when she'd first seen it, over six years ago. She'd come to the Cape after the conviction had been set aside. The District Attorney hadn't pressed for a new trial because Rob Legler, his vital prosecution witness, had disappeared.

She'd fled here, completely across the continent—as far away from California as she could get; as far away from the people she'd known and the place she'd lived and the college and the whole academic community there. She never wanted to see them again—the friends who had turned out not to be friends but hostile strangers who spoke of "poor Carl" because they blamed his suicide on her too.

She'd come to Cape Cod because she'd always heard that New Englanders and Cape people were reticent and reserved and wanted nothing to do with strangers, and that was good. She needed a place to hide, to find herself, to sort it all out, to try to think through what had happened, to try to come back to life.

She'd cut her hair and dyed it sable brown, and that was enough to make her look completely different from the pictures that had front-paged newspapers all over the country during the trial.

She guessed that only fate could have prompted her to select Ray's real estate office when she went looking for a house to rent. She'd actually made an appointment with another realtor, but on impulse she'd gone in to see him first because she liked his hand-lettered sign and the window boxes that were filled with yellow and champagne mums.

She had waited until he finished with another client—a leathery-faced old man with thick, curling hair—and admired the way Ray advised him to hang on to his property, that he'd find a tenant for the apartment in the house to help carry expenses.

After the old man left she said, "Maybe I'm here at the right time. I want to rent a house."

But he wouldn't even show her the old Hunt place. "The Lookout is too big, too lonesome and too drafty for you," he said. "But I just got in a rental on an authentic Cape in excellent condition that's fully furnished. It can even be bought eventually, if you like it. How much room do you need, Miss . . . Mrs. . . . ?"

"Miss Kiernan," she told him. "Nancy Kiernan." Instinctively she used her mother's maiden name. "Not much, really. I won't be having company or visitors."

She liked the fact that he didn't pry or even look curious. "The Cape is a good place to come when you want to be by yourself," he said. "You can't be lonesome walking on the beach or watching the sunset or just looking out the window in the morning."

Then Ray had brought her up here, and immediately she knew that she would stay. The combination family and dining room had been fashioned from the old keeping room that had once been the heart of the house. She loved the rocking chair in front of the fireplace and the way the table was in front of the windows so that it was possible to eat and look down over the harbor and the bay.

She was able to move in right away, and if Ray wondered why she had absolutely nothing except the two suitcases she'd taken off the bus, he didn't show it. She said that her mother had died and she had sold their home in Ohio and decided to come East. She simply omitted talking about the six years that had lapsed in between.

That night, for the first time in months, she slept through the night—a deep, dreamless sleep in which she didn't hear Peter and Lisa calling her; wasn't in the courtroom listening to Carl condemn her.

That first morning here, she'd made coffee and sat by the window. It had been a clear, brilliant day—the cloudless sky purple-blue; the bay tranquil and still; the only movement the arc of sea gulls hovering near the fishing boats.

With her fingers wrapped around the coffee cup, she'd sipped and watched. The warmth of the coffee had flowed through her body. The sunbeams had warmed her face. The tranquillity of the scene enhanced the calming sense of peace that the long, dreamless sleep had begun.

Peace . . . give me peace. That had been her prayer during the trial; in prison. *Let me learn to accept.* Seven years ago . . .

Nancy sighed, realizing that she was still standing by the bottom step of the staircase. It was so easy to get lost in remembering. That was why she tried so hard to live each day . . . not look back or into the future.

She began to go upstairs slowly. How could there ever be peace for her, knowing that if Rob Legler ever showed up they'd try her again for murder; take her away from Ray and Missy and Michael? For an instant, she dropped her face into her hands. *Don't think about it,* she told herself. *It's no use.*

At the head of the stairs she shook her head determinedly and walked quickly into the master bedroom. She threw open the windows and shivered as the wind blew the curtains back against her. Clouds were starting to form, and the water in the bay had begun to churn with whitecaps. The temperature was dropping rapidly. Nancy was enough of a Cape person now to know that a cold wind like this usually blew in a storm.

But it really was still clear enough to have the children out. She liked them to have as much fresh air as possible in the morning. After lunch, Missy napped and Michael went to kindergarten.

She started to pull the sheets from the big double bed and hesitated. Missy had been sniffling yesterday. Should she go down and warn her not to unzip the neck of her jacket? It was one of her favorite tricks. Missy always complained that all her clothes felt too tight at the neck.

Nancy deliberated an instant, then pulled the sheets completely back and off the bed. Missy had on a turtleneck shirt. Her throat would be covered even if she undid the button. Besides, it would take only ten or fifteen minutes to strip and change the beds and turn on a wash.

Ten minutes at the most, Nancy promised herself, to quiet the nagging feeling of worry that was insistently telling her to go out to the children *now*.

2

Some mornings Jonathan Knowles walked to the drugstore to pick up his morning paper. Other days he pedaled on his bike. His outing always took him past the old Nickerson house, the one that Ray Eldredge had bought when he married the pretty girl who was renting it.

When old Sam Nickerson had had the place it had begun to be rundown, but now it looked snug and solid. Ray had put on a new roof and had painted the trim, and his wife certainly had a green thumb. The yellow and orange mums in the window boxes gave a cheerful warmth even to the bleakest day.

In nice weather, Nancy Eldredge was often out early in the morning working on her garden. She always had a pleasant greeting for him and then went back to her work. Jonathan admired that trait in a woman. He'd known Ray's folks when they were summer people up here. Of course, the Eldredges had helped settle the Cape. Ray's father had told Jonathan the whole family line right back to the one who had come over on the *Mayflower*.

The fact that Ray shared enough love for the Cape to decide to build his business career here was particularly exemplary in Jonathan's eyes. The Cape had lakes and ponds and the bay and the ocean. It had woods to walk in, and land for people to spread out on. And it was a good place for a young couple to raise children. It was a good place to retire and live out the end of your life. Jonathan and Emily had always spent vacations here and looked forward to the day when they'd be able to stay here the year around. They'd almost made it, too. But for Emily it wasn't to be.

Jonathan sighed. He was a big man, with thick white hair and a broad face that was beginning to fold into jowls. A retired lawyer, he'd found inactivity depressing. You couldn't do much fishing in the winter. And poking around antique stores and refinishing furniture wasn't the fun it had been when Emily was with him. But in this second year of his permanent residency at the Cape, he'd started to write a book.

Begun as a hobby, it had become an absorbing daily activity. A publisher friend had read a few chapters of it one weekend and promptly sent him a contract. The book was a case study of famous murder trials. Jonathan worked on it five hours every day, seven days a week, starting promptly at nine-thirty in the morning.

The wind bit against him. He pulled out his muffler, grateful for the watery sunshine he felt on his face as he glanced in the direction of the bay. With the shrubbery stripped, you could see clear to the water. Only the old Hunt house on its high bluff interrupted the view—the house they called The Lookout.

Jonathan always looked at the bay right at this point of his trip. This morning again, he squinted as he turned his head. Irritated, he looked back at the road after barely registering the stormy, churning whitecaps. That fellow who rented the house must have something metallic in the window, he thought. It was a damn nuisance. He felt like asking Ray to mention it to him, then ruefully brushed the thought away. The tenant might just suggest that Jonathan check the bay somewhere else along the way.

He shrugged unconsciously. He was directly in front of the Eldredge house, and Nancy was sitting at the breakfast table by the window talking to the little boy. The little girl was on her lap.

Jonathan glanced away quickly, feeling like an intruder and not wanting to catch her eye. Oh, well, he'd get the paper, fix his solitary breakfast and get to his desk. Today he'd begin working on the Harmon murder case—the one that he suspected would make the most interesting chapter of all.

3

Ray pushed open the door of his office, unable to shake the nagging sensation of worry that like an unlocated toothache was throbbing somewhere inside him. What was the matter? It was more than just making Nancy acknowledge her birthday and risking the memories it aroused. Actually, she'd been pretty calm. He knew her well enough to understand when the tension was building about that other life.

It could be triggered by something like the sight of a dark-haired boy and girl together who were the ages of her other children, or a discussion of the murder of that little girl who'd been found dead in Cohasset last year. But Nancy was all right this morning. It was something else—a feeling of foreboding.

"Oh, no! What does that mean?"

Ray looked up, startled. Dorothy was at her desk. Her hair, more gray than brown, casually framed her long, pleasant face. Her sensible beige sweater and brown tweed skirt had an almost studied dowdiness and signaled the wearer's indifference to frills.

Dorothy had been Ray's first client when he had opened this office. The girl he had hired didn't show up, and Dorothy had volunteered to help him out for a few days. She'd been with him ever since.

"You do realize that you're shaking your head and frowning," she told him.

Ray smiled sheepishly. "Just morning jitters, I guess. How are you doing?"

Dorothy immediately became businesslike. "Fine. I have the file all together on The Lookout. What time do you expect that fellow who wants to see it?"

"Around two," Ray told her. He bent over her desk. "Where did you ever dig out those plans?"

"They're on file in the library. Don't forget, that house was begun in sixteen-ninety. It would make a marvelous restaurant. If anyone is willing to spend money renovating it, it could be a showcase. And you can't beat that waterfront location."

"I gather Mr. Kragopoulos and his wife have built up and sold several restaurants and don't mind spending the dollars to do every-thing the way it should be done."

"I've never yet met a Greek who couldn't make a go of a restau-rant," Dorothy commented as she closed the file.

"And all Englishmen are fags and no German has a sense of humor and most Puerto Ricans—I mean Spics—are on welfare. . . . God, I hate labels!" Ray took his pipe from his breast pocket and jammed it into his mouth.

"What?" Dorothy looked up at him bewildered. "I certainly was not labeling—or I guess, maybe I was, but not in the way you took it." She turned her back to him as she put the file away, and Ray stalked into his private office and closed the door.

He had hurt her. Stupidly, unnecessarily. What in the hell was the matter with him? Dorothy was the most decent, fair-minded, non-biased person he knew. What a lousy thing to say to her. Sigh-ing, he reached for the humidor on his desk and filled his pipe. He puffed thoughtfully on it for fifteen minutes before he dialed Dorothy's extension.

"Yes." Her voice was constrained when she picked up the phone.

"Are the girls in yet?"

"Yes."

"Coffee made?"

"Yes." Dorothy did not ask him if he was ready to have some.

"Would you mind bringing yours in here and a cup for me? And ask the girls to hold calls for fifteen minutes."

"All right." Dorothy hung up.

Ray got up to open the door for her, and when she came in with the steaming cups he carefully closed it.

"Peace," he said contritely. "I'm terribly sorry."

"I believe that," Dorothy said, "and it's all right, but what's the matter?"

"Sit down, please." Ray gestured to the rust-colored leather chair by his desk. He took his coffee to the window and stared moodily out at the graying landscape.

"How would you like to come to our house for dinner tonight?" he asked. "We're celebrating Nancy's birthday."

He heard her sharp intake of breath and spun around. "Do you think it's a mistake?"

Dorothy was the only one on the Cape who knew about Nancy. Nancy herself had told her and asked her advice before she had agreed to marry Ray.

Dorothy's voice and eyes were speculative as she answered. "I don't know, Ray. What's the thinking behind a celebration?"

"The thinking is that you can't pretend that Nancy doesn't have birthdays! Of course, it's more than just that. It's that Nancy has got to break with the past, to stop hiding."

"*Can* she break with the past? *Can* she stop hiding with the prospect of another murder trial always hanging over her?"

"But that's just it. The *prospect*. Dorothy, do you realize that that fellow who testified against her hasn't been seen or heard of

for over six years? God knows where he is now or if he's even alive.
For all we know, he's sneaked back into this country under another
name and is just as anxious as Nancy not to start the whole business
up. Don't forget, he's officially a deserter from the Army. There's a
pretty stiff penalty waiting for him if he's caught."

"That's probably true," Dorothy agreed.

"It is true. And take it one step further. Level with me, now.
What do people in this town think of Nancy?—and I include the
girls in my own office here."

Dorothy hesitated. "They think she's very pretty . . . they admire
the way she wears clothes . . . they say she's always pleasant . . . and
they think she keeps to herself pretty much."

"That's a nice way of putting it. I've heard cracks about my wife
thinking she's 'too good for the folks around here.' At the club I'm
getting more and more ribbing about why I only have a golf mem-
bership and why I don't bring that beautiful wife of mine around.
Last week Michael's school called and asked if Nancy would consider working on some committee. Needless to say, she turned
them down. Last month I finally got her to go to the realtors' dinner, and when they took the group picture, she was in the ladies'
room."

"She's afraid of being recognized."

"I understand that. But don't you see that that possibility gets
less likely all the time? And even if someone said to her, 'You're
a dead ringer for that girl from California who was accused' . . .
well, you know what I mean, Dorothy. For most people it would
end there. A resemblance. Period. God, remember that guy who
used to pose for all those whiskey and bank ads, the one who was
a ringer for Lyndon Johnson? I was in the Army with his nephew.
People do look like other people. It's that simple. And if there ever
is another trial, I want Nancy to be entrenched with the people
here. I want them to feel she's one of them and that they're rooting

for her. Because after she's acquitted, she'll have to come here and take up life again. We all will."

"And if there's a trial and she isn't acquitted?"

"I simply won't consider that possibility," Ray said flatly. "How about it? Have we got a date tonight?"

"I'd like very much to come," Dorothy said. "And I agree with most of what you've said."

"Most?"

"Yes." She looked at him steadily. "I think you've got to ask yourself how much of this sudden desire to opt for a more normal life is just for Nancy and how much because of other motives."

"Meaning what?"

"Ray, I was here when the Secretary of State of Massachusetts urged you to go into politics because the Cape needs young men of your caliber to represent it. I heard him say that he'd give you any help and endorsement possible. It's pretty hard not to be able to take him up on that. But as things stand now, you can't. And you know it."

Dorothy left the room without giving him a chance to answer. Ray finished the coffee and sat down at his desk. The anger and irritation and tension drained from him, and he felt depressed and ashamed of himself. She was right, of course. He did want to pretend that there wasn't any threat hanging over them, that everything was just nifty. And he had a hell of a nerve, too. He'd known what he was getting into when he'd married Nancy. If he hadn't, she certainly had pointed it out. She'd done her best to warn him.

Ray stared unseeingly at the mail on his desk, thinking of the times in the last few months when he'd blown up unreasonably at Nancy just the way he had this morning at Dorothy. Like the way he had acted when she had shown him the watercolor she'd done of the house. She should study art. Even now she was good enough to exhibit locally. He'd said, "It's very good. Now which closet are you going to hide it in?"

Nancy had looked so stricken, so defenseless. He'd wanted to bite his tongue off. He'd said, "Honey, I'm so sorry. It's just that I'm so proud of you. I want you to show it off."

How many of these flare-ups were being caused because he was tired of the constant constriction on their activities?

He sighed and started going through his mail.

At quarter past ten, Dorothy threw open the door of his office. Her usually healthy pink complexion was a sickly grayish white. He jumped up to go to her. But shaking her head, she pushed the door closed behind her and held out the paper she'd been hiding under her arm.

It was the weekly *Cape Cod Community News*. Dorothy had it open to the second section, the one that always featured a human-interest story. She dropped it on his desk.

Together they stared down at the large picture that to anyone was unmistakably Nancy. It was one he'd never seen before, in her tweed suit, with her hair pulled back and already darkened. The caption under it said, CAN THIS BE A HAPPY BIRTHDAY FOR NANCY HARMON? Another picture showed Nancy leaving the courtroom during her trial, her face wooden and expressionless, her hair cascading down her shoulders. A third picture was a copy of a snapshot of Nancy with her arms around two young children.

The first line of the story read: "Somewhere today Nancy Harmon is celebrating her 32nd birthday and the seventh anniversary of the death of the children she was found guilty of murdering."

4

It was timing. The whole universe existed because of split-second timing. Now his timing would be perfect. Hurriedly, he backed the station wagon out of the garage. It was such a cloudy day it had been hard to see much through the telescope, but he could tell that she'd been putting the children's coats on.

He felt in his pocket and the needles were there — filled, ready to use, to produce instant unconsciousness; dreamless, absolute sleep.

He could feel the perspiration starting under his arms and in his groin, and great beads of it were forming on his forehead and rolling down his cheeks. That was bad. It was a cold day. Mustn't look excited or nervous.

He took a precious few seconds to dab his face with the old towel he kept on the front seat and glanced over his shoulder. The canvas raincoat was the kind many Cape men kept in their cars, especially around fishing season; so were the rods that showed against the back window. But that coat was big enough to cover two small children. He giggled excitedly and swung the car toward Route 6A.

Wiggins' Market was on the corner of this road and Route 6A. Whenever he was at the Cape he shopped there. Of course, he brought most of the staples he needed with him whenever he came to stay. It was too risky to go out much. There was always the chance that he'd run into Nancy and she'd recognize him even with his changed appearance. It had almost happened four years ago. He'd been in a supermarket in Hyannis Port and he'd heard her voice behind him. He was reaching for a jar of coffee, and her hand went right up next to his as she took a jar from the same shelf. She was saying, "Wait a minute, Mike. I want to get something here," and while he froze, she brushed against him and murmured "Oh, I'm sorry."

He didn't dare to answer—just stood there—and she moved on. He was positive she hadn't even looked at him. But after that he had never risked a meeting. It was necessary, though, for him to establish a casual routine in Adams Port, because someday it might be important for people to dismiss his comings and goings as routine. That was why he bought milk and bread and meat at Wiggins' Market always about ten in the morning. Nancy never left the house before eleven, and even then she always went to Lowery's Market, down the road a half mile. And the Wigginses had begun to greet him as a customer of long standing. Well, he'd be there in a few minutes, right on schedule.

There wasn't anyone out walking at all. The raw wind was probably discouraging any inclination to go outdoors. He was almost to Route 6A and slowed to a full stop.

The incredible luck. There wasn't a car in either direction. Quickly he accelerated, and the station wagon shot across the main street and onto the road that ran along the back of the Eldredge property. Audacity—that was all it took. Any fool could try to come up with a foolproof plan. But to have a plan so simple that it was unbelievable even to call it a plan—a schedule timed to the split second—that was real genius. To willingly leave yourself open to failure—to tightrope-walk across a dozen pits so that when the act was accomplished no one even glanced in your direction—that was the way.

Ten minutes of ten. The children had probably been out one minute now. Oh, he knew the possibilities. One of them might have gone into the house to the bathroom or for a drink of water, but not likely, not likely. Every day for a month straight he'd watched them. Unless it was actually raining, they came out to play. She never came to check them for ten to fifteen minutes. They never went back into the house for those same ten minutes.

Nine minutes of ten. He steered the car into the dirt road on their property. The community paper would be delivered in a few minutes. That article would be out today. Motivation for Nancy to explode into violence . . . exposure of her part . . . all the people in this town talking in shocked tones, walking by this house, staring . . .

He stopped the car halfway into the woods. No one could see it from the road. She couldn't see it from the house. He got out quickly and, keeping close to the protection of the trees, hurried to the children's play area. The leaves were off most of the trees, but there were enough pines and other evergreens to shield him.

He could hear the children's voices before he saw them. The boy, his voice panting a little—he must be pushing the girl on the swing . . . "We'll ask Daddy what to buy for Mommy. I'll take both our money."

The girl laughed. "Good, Mike, good. Higher, Mike—push me higher, please."

He stole up behind the boy, who heard him in that last second. He had an impression of startled blue eyes and a mouth that rounded in terror before he covered both with one hand and with the other plunged the needle through the woolen mitten. The boy tried to pull away, stiffened, then crumpled noiselessly to the ground.

The swing was coming back—the girl calling, "Push, Mike—don't stop pushing." He caught the swing by the right side chain, stopped it and encircled the small, uncomprehending wiggly body.

Carefully stifling the soft cry, he plunged the other needle through the red mitten that had a smiling kitten face sewn on the back. An instant later, the girl sighed and slumped against him.

He didn't notice that one mitten caught on the swing and was pulled off as he easily lifted both children in his arms and ran to the car.

At five minutes of ten they were crumpled under the canvas raincoat. He backed down the dirt road and onto the paved highway behind Nancy's property. He cursed as he saw a small Dodge sedan coming toward him. It slowed up slightly to let him pull into the right lane, and he turned his head away.

Damn the luck. As he passed, he managed a swift sidelong glance at the driver of the other car and got an impression of a sharp nose and thin chin silhouetted from under a shapeless hat. The other driver didn't seem to turn his head at all.

He had a fleeting feeling of familiarity: probably someone from the Cape, but maybe not aware that the station wagon he had slowed up for had come off the narrow dirt road leading from the Eldredge property. Most people weren't observant. In a few minutes this man probably wouldn't even have a recollection of having slowed for an instant to let a car complete a turn.

He watched the Dodge through the rearview mirror until it disappeared. With a grunt of satisfaction, he adjusted the mirror so that it reflected the canvas raincoat on the back deck. It was apparently tossed casually over fishing gear. Satisfied, he flipped the mirror back into place without looking into it again. If he had looked into it, he would have seen that the car he had just been watching was slowing, backing up.

At four minutes past ten he walked into Wiggins' Market and grunted a greeting as he reached into the refrigerator section for a quart of milk.

5

Nancy came down the steep staircase precariously balancing an armful of towels and sheets, pajamas and underwear. On impulse she'd decided to do a wash that could be hung outdoors to dry before the storm broke. Winter was here. It was on the edge of the yard, forcing the last few dead leaves off the trees. It was settling into the dirt road that now was as hardened as concrete. It was changing the color of the bay into a smoky gray-blue.

Outside, the storm was building, but now, while there was still some weak sun, she'd take advantage of it. She loved the fresh smell of sheets dried outside; loved to pull them against her face as she drifted off to sleep with the way they captured the faint scent of cranberry bogs and pine and the salty smell of the sea—so different from the coarse, rough, dank smell of prison sheets. She pushed the thought away.

At the foot of the staircase she started to turn in the direction of the back door, then stopped. How foolish. The children were fine. They'd been out only fifteen minutes, and this frantic anxiety that was her constant albatross had to be conquered. Even now she suspected that Missy sensed it and was beginning to respond to her overprotection. She'd turn the wash on, then call them in. While they watched their ten-thirty television program, she'd have a second cup of coffee and look at the weekly *Cape Cod Community*

News. With the season over, there might be some good antiques available and not at tourist prices. She wanted an old-fashioned set-tee for the parlor—the high-backed kind they used to call a "settle" in the seventeen-hundreds.

In the laundry room off the kitchen she sorted the wash, tossed the sheets and towels into the machine, added detergent and bleach and finally pushed the button to start the cycle.

Now it surely was time to call the children. But at the front door she detoured. The paper had just arrived. The delivery boy was disappearing around the curve in the road. She picked it up, shiv-ering against the increasing wind, and hurried into the kitchen. She turned the burner jet under the still-warm coffeepot. Then, anxious to get a look at the classified page, she thumbed quickly to the second section of the paper.

Her eyes focused on the blaring headline and the pictures—all the pictures: of her and Carl and Rob Legler; the one of her with Peter and Lisa . . . that clinging, trusting way they'd always huddled up to her. Through a roaring in her ears she remembered vividly the time they'd posed for that one. Carl had taken it.

"Don't pay attention to me," he'd said; "pretend I'm not here." But they'd known he was there and had shrunk against her, and she had looked down at them as he snapped the picture. Her hands were touching their silky, dark heads.

"No . . . no . . . no . . . no . . . !" Now her body arched in pain. Unsteadily she reached out her hand, and it hit the coffeepot, knocking it over. She drew it back, only dimly feeling the searing liquid that splattered on her fingers.

She had to burn the paper. Michael and Missy mustn't see it. That was it. She'd burn the paper so that no one could see it. She ran to the fireplace in the dining room.

The fireplace . . . that wasn't cheery and warm and protect-ing anymore. Because there was no haven . . . there never could be a haven for her. She squeezed the paper together and reached unsteadily for the box of matches on the mantel. A wisp of smoke and a flame, and then the paper began to burn as she stuffed it between the logs.

Everyone on the Cape was reading that paper. They'd know . . . they'd all know. The one picture they'd surely recognize. She didn't even remember that anyone had seen her after she'd cut her hair and dyed it. The paper was burning brightly now. She watched as the picture with Peter and Lisa flamed, and charred and curled. Dead, both of them; and she'd be better off with them. There was no place to hide for her . . . or to forget. Ray could take care of Michael and Missy. Tomorrow in Michael's class the children would be looking at him, whispering, pointing their fingers.

The children. She must save the children. No, *get* the children. That was it. They'd catch cold.

She stumbled to the back door and pulled it open. "Peter . . . Lisa . . ." she called. No, no! It was Michael and Missy. *They* were her children.

"Michael. Missy. Come here. Come in now!" Her wail heightened to a shriek. Where were they? She hurried out to the backyard, unmindful of the cold that bit through her light sweater.

The swing. They must have gotten off the swing. They were probably in the woods. "Michael. Missy. Michael! Missy! Don't hide! Come here now!"

The swing was still moving. The wind was making it sway. Then she saw the mitten. Missy's mitten, caught in the metal loops of the swing.

From far off she heard a sound. What sound? The children.

The lake! They must be at the lake. They weren't supposed to go there, but maybe they had. They'd be found. Like the others. In the water. Their faces wet and swollen and still.

She grabbed Missy's mitten, the mitten with the smile face, and staggered toward the lake. She called their names over and over again. She pushed her way through the woods and out onto the sandy beach.

In the lake a little way out, something was glistening below the surface. Was it something red . . . another mitten . . . Missy's hand? She plunged into the icy water as far as her shoulders and reached down. But there wasn't anything there. Frantically Nancy clutched her fingers together so that they formed a strainer, but there was nothing—only the terrible numbing cold water. She looked down, trying to see to the bottom; leaned over and fell. The water gushed into her nostrils and mouth and burned her face and neck.

Somehow she staggered up and back before her wet clothes pulled her down again. She fell onto the ice-crusted sand. Through the roar in her ears and the mist that was closing in front of her eyes, she looked into the woods and saw him—his face . . . *Whose* face?

The mist closed over her eyes completely. Sounds died away: the mournful cackle of the sea gull . . . the lapping of the water . . . Silence.

It was there that Ray and Dorothy found her. Shivering uncontrollably, lying on the sand, her hair and clothes plastered to her head and body, her eyes blank and uncomprehending, angry blisters raised on the hand that clutched a small red mitten to her cheek.

6

Jonathan carefully washed and rinsed his breakfast dishes, scoured the omelet pan and swept the kitchen floor. Emily had been naturally, effortlessly neat, and years of living with her had made him appreciate the intrinsic comfort of tidiness. He always hung his clothes in the closets, put his laundry in the bathroom hamper and cleared up immediately after his solitary meals. He even had an eye for the kind of detail that his cleaning woman missed and after she left on Wednesdays would do small jobs like washing canisters and bric-a-brac and polishing surfaces that she'd left cloudy with wax.

In New York he and Emily had lived on Sutton Place, on the southeast corner of Fifty-fifth Street. Their apartment building had extended over the FDR Drive to the edge of the East River. Sometimes they had sat on their seventeenth-floor balcony and watched the lights of the bridges that spanned the river and talked about the time when they'd be retired at the Cape and looking out over Maushop Lake.

"You won't have Bertha in every day to keep the wheels spinning," he'd teased her.

"By the time we get up there, Bertha will be ready to retire and I'll break you in as my assistant. All we'll really need is a weekly cleaning woman. How about you? Will you miss having a car pick you up at the door anytime you want it?"

Jonathan had answered that he'd decided to buy a bicycle. "I'd do it now," he'd told Emily, "but I'm afraid some of our clients might get upset if the word was around that I arrived at work on a ten-speeder."

"And you'll try your hand at writing," Emily had prodded. "I sometimes wish you'd just taken a chance and done it years ago."

"Never could afford to, married to you," he'd said. "The one-woman war against recession. All Fifth Avenue stays in the black when Mrs. Knowles goes shopping."

"It's your fault," she'd retorted. "You're always telling me to spend your money."

"I like spending it on you," he'd told her, "and I have no complaints. I've been lucky."

If only they'd had even a few years up here together . . . Jonathan sighed and hung up the dish towel. Seeing Nancy Eldredge and her children framed in the window this morning had vaguely depressed him. Maybe it was the weather or the long winter setting in, but he was restless, apprehensive. Something was bothering him. It was the kind of itch he used to get when he was preparing a brief and some facts just didn't jibe.

Well, he'd get to his desk. He was anxious to start working on the Harmon chapter.

He could have taken early retirement, he thought, as he walked slowly into his study. As it turned out, that was just what he had done anyway. The minute he lost Emily, he'd sold the New York apartment, put in his resignation, pensioned off Bertha and, like a dog licking its wounds, had come here to this house that they'd picked out together. After the first bleak grief, he'd found a measure of contentment.

Now writing the book was a fascinating and absorbing experience. When he'd gotten the idea for doing it, he had asked Kevin Parks, a meticulous free-lance researcher and old friend, to come up for a weekend. Then he had outlined his plan to him. Jonathan had selected ten controversial criminal trials. He'd proposed that Kev take on the job of putting together a file of all available material on those trials: court transcripts; depositions; newspaper accounts; pictures; gossip—anything he could find. Jonathan planned to study each file thoroughly and then decide how to write the chapter—either agreeing with the verdict or rejecting it, and giving his reasons. He was calling the book "Verdict in Doubt."

He'd already finished three chapters. The first was called "The Sam Sheppard Trial." His opinion: not guilty. Too many loopholes; too much suppressed evidence. Jonathan agreed with the Dorothy Kilgallen opinion that the jury had found Sam Sheppard guilty of adultery, not murder.

The second chapter was "The Cappolino Trial." Marge Farger, in his opinion, belonged in a prison cell with her former boyfriend.

The just-completed chapter was "The Edgar Smith Trial." Jonathan's view was that Edgar Smith was guilty but deserved his freedom. Fourteen years constituted a life sentence today, and he had rehabilitated and educated himself in a grisly cell on Death Row.

Now he sat down at his massive desk and reached into the file drawer for the thick cardboard folders that had arrived the previous day. They were labeled THE HARMON CASE.

A note from Kevin was stapled to the first envelope. It read:

Jon, I have a hunch you'll enjoy getting your teeth into this one. The defendant was a sitting duck for the prosecutor; even her husband broke down on the stand and practically accused her in front of the jury. If they ever locate the missing prosecution witness and try her again, she'd better have a stronger story than last time. The District Attorney's office out there knows where she is, but I couldn't get it from them; somewhere in the East is the best I can do.

Jonathan opened the file with the accelerating pulse that he always associated with the beginning of an interesting new case. He never allowed himself to do much speculating until he got the research all together, but his memory of this case when it was being tried six or seven years ago made him curious. He remembered how at that time just reading the trial testimony had left so many questions in his mind . . . questions he wanted to concentrate on now. He recalled that his overall impression of the Harmon case was that Nancy Harmon never had told all she knew about the disappearance of her children.

He reached into the folder and began to lay out the meticulously labeled items on the desk. There were pictures of Nancy Harmon taken during her trial. She certainly was a pretty little thing with that waist-length hair. According to the papers she was twenty-five at the time the murders were committed. She looked even younger—not much more than a teenager. The dresses she wore were so youthful . . . almost childish . . . they added to the overall effect. Probably her attorney had suggested that she look as young as possible.

Funny, but ever since he'd started planning this book he'd felt that he'd seen that girl somewhere. He stared at the pictures in front of him. Of course. She looked like a younger version of Ray Eldredge's wife! That explained the nagging resemblance. The expression was totally different, but wouldn't it be a small world if there was some family relationship?

His eye fell on the first typewritten page, which gave a rundown on Nancy Harmon. She had been born in California and raised in Ohio. Well, that let out any possibility of her being a close relative to Nancy Eldredge. Ray's wife's family had been neighbors of Dorothy Prentiss in Virginia.

Dorothy Prentiss. He felt a quick dart of pleasure at the thought of the handsome woman who worked with Ray. Jonathan often stopped by their office around five o'clock, when he picked up the evening paper, the *Boston Globe*. Ray had suggested some interesting land investments to him, and they had all proved sound. He'd also persuaded Jonathan to become active in the town, and as a result they'd become good friends.

Still, Jonathan realized that he went into Ray's office more often than necessary. Ray would say, "You're just in time for an end-of-the-day drink" and call out to Dorothy to join them.

Emily had liked daiquiris. Dorothy always had Jonathan's favorite drink—a Rob Roy with a twist. The three of them would sit for a half hour or so in Ray's private office.

Dorothy had a penetrating humor that he enjoyed. Her family had been show-business people, and she had countless great stories about traveling with them. She'd planned a career too, but after three small parts Off Broadway she had gotten married and settled down in Virginia. After her husband died she'd come up to the Cape planning to open an interior-decorating shop, then had gotten started working with Ray. Ray said that Dorothy was a hell of a real estate saleswoman. She could help people visualize the possibilities in a place, no matter how seedy it looked at first glance.

More and more often lately Jonathan had toyed with the idea of suggesting that Dorothy join him for dinner. Sundays were long, and a couple of Sunday afternoons recently he'd actually started to dial her number, then stopped. He didn't want to rush into getting involved with someone he'd run into constantly. And he just wasn't sure. Maybe she came on a little too strong for him. All those years of living with Emily's total femininity had made him somewhat unprepared for reacting on a personal level to a terribly independent woman.

God, what was the matter with him? He was so easily diverted into woolgathering this morning. Why was he letting himself get distracted from this Harmon case?

Resolutely he lit his pipe, picked up the file and leaned back in his chair. Deliberately he picked up the first batch of papers.

An hour and fifteen minutes passed. The silence was unbroken except for the ticking of the clock, the increasing insistence of the wind through the pines outside his window and Jonathan's occasional snort of disbelief. Finally, frowning in concentration, he laid the papers down and walked slowly to the kitchen to make coffee. Something smelled about that whole Harmon trial. From as much of the transcript as he'd read through so far it was evident that there was something fishy there . . . an undercurrent that made it impossible for the facts to hang together in any kind of reasonably cohesive way.

He went into the immaculate kitchen and absently half-filled the kettle. While he waited for it to heat, he walked to the front door. The *Cape Cod Community News* was already on the porch. Tucking it under his arm, he went back into the kitchen, poured a rounded teaspoon of Taster's Choice into a cup, added the boiling water, stirred and began to sip as with the other hand he turned the pages of the paper, scanning the contents.

He had almost finished the coffee when he got to the second section. His hand with the cup stopped in mid-air as his gaze froze on the picture of Ray Eldredge's wife.

In that first instant of realization, Jonathan sadly accepted two irrefutable facts: Dorothy Prentiss had deliberately lied to him about having known Nancy as a child in Virginia; and retired or not, he should have been enough of a lawyer to trust his own instincts. Subconsciously, he had always suspected that Nancy Harmon and Nancy Eldredge were one and the same person.

7

It was so cold. There was a gritty taste in her mouth. Sand—why? Where was she?

She could hear Ray calling her, feel him bending over her, cradling her against him. "Nancy, what's the matter? Nancy, where are the children?"

She could hear the fear in his voice. She tried to raise her hand, then felt it fall loosely by her side. She tried to speak, but no words formed on her lips. Ray was there, but she couldn't reach him.

She heard Dorothy say, "Pick her up, Ray. Take her to the house. We have to get help looking for the children."

The children. They must find them. Nancy wanted to tell Ray to look for them. She felt her lips trying to form words, but the words wouldn't come.

"Oh, my God!" She heard the break in Ray's voice. She wanted to say, "Don't bother with me; don't bother with me. Look for the children." But she couldn't speak. She felt him pick her up and hold her against him. "What's happened to her, Dorothy?" he asked. "What's the matter with her?"

"Ray, we've got to call the police."

"The police!" Vaguely Nancy could hear the resistance in his voice.

"Of course. We need help finding the children. Ray, hurry!

Every moment is precious. Don't you see—you can't protect Nancy now. Everyone will know her from that picture."

The picture. Nancy felt herself being carried. Remotely she knew she was shivering. But that wasn't what she had to think about. It was the picture of her in the tweed suit she'd bought after the conviction was overturned. They'd taken her out of prison and brought her to court. The state hadn't tried her again. Carl was dead, and the student who'd testified against her had disappeared, and so she'd been released.

The prosecuting attorney had said to her, "Don't think this is over. If I spend the rest of my life, I'll find a way to get a conviction that sticks." And with his words beating against her, she'd left the courtroom.

Afterward, when she'd received permission to leave the state, she'd had her hair cut and dyed and gone shopping. She had always hated the kind of clothes Carl liked her to wear and had bought the three-piece suit and brown turtleneck sweater. She still wore the jacket and slacks; she'd worn them shopping only last week. That was another reason the picture was so recognizable. The picture . . . it had been taken in the bus terminal; that was where she'd been.

She hadn't known that anyone was taking a picture of her. She'd left on the last evening bus for Boston. The terminal hadn't been crowded, and no one had paid any attention to her. She'd really thought that she could just slip away and try to begin again. But someone had just been waiting to start it all over again.

I want to die, she thought. *I want to die.*

Ray was walking swiftly, but trying to shield her with his jacket. The wind was biting through the wet clothes. He couldn't shield her; not even he could shield her. It was too late. . . . Maybe it had always been too late. Peter and Lisa and Michael and Missy. They were all gone. . . . It was too late for all of them.

No. No. No. Michael and Missy. They were here a little while ago. They were playing. They were out on the swing and then the mitten was there. Michael wouldn't leave Missy. He was so careful of her. It was like last time. Last time, and they'd find them the way they found Peter and Lisa, with the wet seaweed and bits of plastic on their faces and in their hair and their bodies swollen.

They must be at the house. Dorothy was opening the door and saying, "I'll call the police, Ray."

Nancy felt the darkness coming at her. She began sliding back and away. . . . No . . . no . . . no. . . .

8

Oh, the activity. Oh, the way they were all scurrying around like ants—all milling around her house and yard. He licked his lips anxiously. They were so dry when all the rest of him was wet—his hands and feet and groin and underarms. Perspiration was streaming down his neck and back.

As soon as he got back to the big house, he carried the children in and brought them right up to the room with the telescope. He could keep an eye on them here and talk to them when they woke up and touch them.

Maybe he'd give the little girl a bath and dry her off in a nice soft towel and rub baby powder on her and kiss her. He had all day to spend with the children. All day; the tide wouldn't come in until seven tonight. By then it would be dark, and no one would be nearby to see or hear. It would be days before they'd be washed in. It would be like last time.

It was so much more enjoyable touching them when he knew their mother was being questioned by now. "What did you do with your children?" they'd ask her.

He watched more police cars swarm up the dirt road into her backyard. But some of them were passing the house. Why were so many of them going to Maushop Lake? Of course. They thought she had taken the children there.

He felt wonderfully gratified. Here he could see everything that was happening without risk, perfectly safe and comfortable. He wondered if Nancy was crying. She had never cried once at her trial until the very end—after the judge sentenced her to the gas chamber. She'd begun sobbing and buried her face in her hands to cover the sound. The court attendants had snapped handcuffs on her, and her long hair had spilled forward, covering the tearstained face that looked hopelessly out at the hostile faces.

He remembered the first time he'd seen her walking across the campus. He'd been immediately attracted to her—the way the wind blew her strawberry-gold hair around her shoulders; the delicately formed face; the small, even white teeth; the enchanting round blue eyes that looked gravely out from thick, sooty brows and lashes.

He heard a sob. Nancy? But of course not. It was coming from the girl. Nancy's child. He turned from the telescope and stared resentfully. But his expression changed to a smile as he studied her. Those damp ringlets on her forehead; the tiny, straight nose; the fair skin . . . she looked a lot like Nancy. Now she wailed as she started to wake up. Well, it was just about time for the drug to wear off; they'd been unconscious nearly an hour.

Regretfully, he left the telescope. He'd laid the children on opposite ends of the musty-smelling velour couch. The little girl was crying in earnest now. "Mommy . . . Mommy." Her eyes were squeezed shut. Her mouth was open. . . . Her little tongue was so pink! Tears were running down her cheeks.

He sat her up and unzipped her jacket. She shrank away from him. "There, there," he said soothingly. "It's all right."

The boy stirred and woke up too. His eyes were startled, just as they had been when he had seen him in the yard. Now he sat up slowly. "Who are you?" he demanded. He rubbed his eyes, shook his head and looked around. "Where are we?"

An articulate child . . . well spoken . . . his voice clear and well modulated. That was good. Well-trained children were easier to handle. Didn't make a fuss. Taught respect for older people, they tended to be pliable. Like the others. They'd come with him so quietly that day. They had knelt in the trunk of the car unquestioningly when he had said they were going to play a game on Mommy.

"It's a game," he told this little boy. "I'm an old friend of your mommy's and she wants to play a birthday game. Did you know it was her birthday today?" He kept patting the little girl while he spoke. She felt so soft and good.

The boy—Michael—looked uncertain. "I don't like this game," he said firmly. Unsteadily he got to his feet. He pushed aside the hands that were touching Missy and reached for her. She clung to him. "Don't cry, Missy," he said soothingly. "It's just a silly game. We'll go home now."

It was obvious that he wasn't going to be fooled easily. The boy had Ray Eldredge's candid expression. "We're not going to play any of your games," he said. "We want to go home."

There was a wonderful way he could make the little boy cooperate. "Let go of your sister," he ordered. "Here, give her to me." He yanked her from the boy. With the other hand he took Michael's wrist and pulled him over to the window. "Do you know what a telescope is?"

Michael nodded uncertainly. "Yes. It's like the glasses my daddy has. It makes things bigger."

"That's right. You're very smart. Now, look in here." The boy put his eye to the viewer. "Now tell me what you see . . . No, squeeze your other eye shut."

"It's looking at my house."

"What do you see there?"

"There are lots of cars . . . police cars. What's the matter?" Alarm made his voice quiver.

He looked down happily at the worried face. A faint pinging sound came from the window. It was starting to sleet. The wind was driving hard little pellets against the glass panes. The visibility would be very poor soon. Even with the telescope it would be hard to see much. But he could have a wonderful time with the children—the whole, long afternoon. And he knew how to make the boy obey. "Do you know what it's like to be dead?" he asked.

"It means to go to God," Michael answered.

He nodded approvingly. "That's right. And this morning your mother went to God. That's why all the police cars are there. Your daddy asked me to mind you for a while and said for you to be good and help me take care of your sister."

Michael looked as though he'd cry too. His lip quivered as he said, "If my mommy went to God, I want to go too."

Running his fingers through Michael's hair, he rocked the still-wailing Missy. "You will," he told him. "Tonight. I promise."

9

The first reports went over the wire-service tickers at noon, in time to make bulletins on the news broadcasts throughout the country. Newscasters, hungering for a story, seized upon it and sent researchers scurrying to the files for records of the Nancy Harmon murder trial.

Publishers chartered planes to send their top crime reporters to Cape Cod.

In San Francisco, two assistant district attorneys listened to the bulletin. One said to the other, "Have I always said that bitch was as guilty as if I'd seen her kill those kids myself? Have I said it? So help me, if they don't hang this one on her, I'll take a leave of absence and personally comb the globe to find that Legler slob and get him back here to testify against her."

In Boston, Dr. Lendon Miles was enjoying the beginning of his lunch break. Mrs. Markley had just left. After a year of intense therapy she was finally beginning to get pretty good insight. She'd made a funny remark a few minutes ago. She'd been discussing an episode from her fourteenth year and said, "Do you realize that thanks to you I'm going through adolescence and change of life all at once? It's a hell of a deal." Only a few months ago she hadn't been doing much joking.

Lendon Miles enjoyed his profession. To him the mind was

a delicate, complicated phenomenon—a mystery that could be unraveled only by a series of infinitely small revelations . . . one leading slowly, patiently into the next. He sighed. His ten-o'clock patient was in early analysis and had been extremely hostile.

He switched on the radio next to his desk to catch the balance of the noon news and was just in time to hear the bulletin.

A shadow of an old pain crossed his face. Nancy Harmon . . . Priscilla's daughter. After fourteen years he could still see Priscilla so clearly: the slender, elegant body; the way she held her head; the smile that came like quicksilver.

She had started working for him a year after her husband's death. She'd been thirty-eight then, two years his junior. Almost immediately he began taking her out to dinner when they worked late, and soon he realized that for the first time in his life the idea of marriage seemed logical and even essential. Until he met Priscilla, work, study, friends and freedom had been enough; he'd simply never met anyone who made him want to alter his status quo.

Gradually she'd told him about herself. Married after her first year in college to an airline pilot, she had one child, a daughter. The marriage had obviously been a happy one. Then on a trip to India her husband had come down with viral pneumonia and had died within twenty-four hours.

"It was so hard to take," Priscilla told him. "Dave flew over a million miles. He brought 707's down in blizzards. And then something so totally unexpected . . . I didn't realize people still died of pneumonia. . . ."

Lendon never did meet Priscilla's daughter. She had left for school in San Francisco soon after Priscilla had come to work for him. Priscilla had talked out her reasons for sending her so far away. "She was growing too close to me," Priscilla had worried. "She's taken Dave's death so hard. I want her to be happy and young and to get away from the whole climate of grief that I think is closing in on us. I went to Auberley and met Dave while I was there. Nancy had been with me to reunions so it isn't as if it's too strange to her."

In November Priscilla had taken a couple of days off to visit Nancy at college. Lendon had driven her to the airport. For a few minutes they had stood in the terminal waiting for her flight to be called. "Of course you know I'll miss you terribly," he'd said.

She was wearing a dark brown suede coat that showed off her patrician blond beauty. "I hope so," she said, and her eyes were clouded. "I'm so worried," she told him. "Nancy's letters are so down lately. I'm just terribly afraid. Did you ever have a feeling of something awful hanging over you?"

Then when he stared at her, they both began to laugh. "You see why I didn't dare mention this before," she said. "I knew you'd think I was crazy."

"On the contrary, my training has taught me to appreciate the value of hunches, only I call it intuition. But why didn't you tell me you were so worried? Maybe I should be going with you. I only wish I'd met Nancy before she left."

"Oh, no. It's probably me being a mother hen. Anyhow, I'll pick your brains when I get back." Somehow their fingers had become entwined.

"Don't worry. Kids all straighten out, and if there are any real problems, I'll fly out over the weekend if you want me."

"I shouldn't bother you. . . ."

An impersonal voice came over the loudspeaker. "Flight Five-six-nine now boarding for San Francisco . . ."

"Priscilla, for God's sake, don't you realize that I love you?"

"I'm glad. . . . I think . . . I know . . . I love you too."

Their last moment together. A beginning . . . a promise of love.

She had called him the next night. To say that she was worried and had to talk to him. She was at dinner with Nancy, but would call as soon as she got back to her hotel. Would he be home?

He waited all night for the call. But it never came. She never got back to the hotel. The next day he learned about the accident. The steering apparatus of the car she'd rented had failed. The car had careened off the road into a ditch.

He probably should have gone to Nancy. But when he finally got through to where she was staying, he spoke to Carl Harmon, the professor who said he and Nancy were planning to marry. He sounded perfectly competent and very much in charge. Nancy wouldn't be returning to Ohio. They had told her mother of their plans at dinner. Mrs. Kiernan had been concerned about Nancy's youth, but that was natural. She would be buried out there, where her husband was interred; the family had, after all, been residents of California for three generations until Nancy was a baby. Nancy was bearing up well. He thought that it was best for them to have a quiet wedding immediately. Nancy should not be alone now.

There had been nothing for Lendon to do. What could he do? Tell Nancy that he and her mother had been falling in love? The odds were that she would simply have resented him. This Professor Harmon sounded fine, and undoubtedly Priscilla had simply been worried about Nancy's taking such a decisive step as marriage at barely eighteen. But surely there was nothing that he, Lendon, could do about that decision.

He'd been glad to accept the offer to teach at the University of London. That was why he'd been out of the country and had never learned of the Harmon murder trial until after it was over.

It was at the University of London that he had met Allison. She was a teacher there, and the sense of sharing that Priscilla had begun to show him had made it impossible to go back to his well-ordered, solitary—selfish—life. From time to time he had wondered where Nancy Harmon had vanished. He'd been living in the Boston area for the last two years, and she was only an hour and a half away. Maybe now he could somehow make up for the way he had failed Priscilla before.

The phone rang. An instant later, the intercom light blinked on his phone. He picked up the receiver. "Mrs. Miles is on the phone, Doctor," his secretary said.

Allison's voice was filled with concern. "Darling, did you by chance hear the news about the Harmon girl?"

"Yes, I did." He had told Allison about Priscilla.

"What are you going to do?"

Her question crystallized the decision he had already made subconsciously. "What I should have done years ago. I'm going to try to help that girl. I'll call you as soon as I can."

"God bless, darling."

Lendon picked up the intercom and spoke crisply to his secretary. "Ask Dr. Marcus to take over my afternoon appointments, please. Tell him it's an emergency. And cancel my four-o'clock class. I'm driving to Cape Cod immediately."

10

"We've started dragging the lake, Ray. We've got bulletins going out on the radio and TV stations, and we're getting manpower from all over to help in the search." Chief Jed Coffin of the Adams Port police tried to adopt the hearty tone that he would normally use if two children were missing.

But even looking at the agony in Ray's eyes and the ashen pallor of his face, it was difficult to sound reassuring and solicitous. Ray had deceived him—introduced him to his wife, talked about her coming from Virginia and having known Dorothy there. He'd filled him with talk and never once told the truth. And the Chief hadn't guessed—or even suspected. That was the real irritation. Not once had he suspected.

To Chief Coffin, what had happened was very clear. That woman had seen the article about herself in the paper, realized that everyone would know who she was and gone berserk. Did to these poor kids the same thing she'd done to her others. Studying Ray shrewdly, he guessed that Ray was thinking pretty much the same thing.

Charred bits of the morning paper were still in the fireplace. The Chief realized Ray was looking at them. From the jagged way the unburned parts were torn, it was obvious they'd been pulled apart by someone in a frenzy.

"Doc Smathers still upstairs with her?" There was unconscious discourtesy in the question. He'd always called Nancy "Mrs. Eldredge" till now.

"Yes. He's going to give her a needle to relax her but not to put her out. We've got to talk to her. Oh, God!"

Ray sat down at the dining-room table and buried his face in his hands. Only a few hours ago Nancy had been sitting in this chair with Missy in her arms and Mike asking, "Is it really your birthday, Mommy?" Had he triggered something in Nancy by demanding she celebrate? . . . And then that article. Had . . . ?

"No!" Ray looked up and blinked, turning his head away from the sight of the policeman standing by the back door.

"What is it?" Chief Coffin asked.

"Nancy is incapable of harming the children. Whatever happened, it wasn't that."

"Your wife when she's herself wouldn't harm them, but I've seen women go off the deep end, and there is the history . . ."

Ray stood up. His hands clenched the edge of the table. His glance went past the Chief, dismissing him. "I need help," he said. "Real help."

The room was in chaos. The police had made a quick search of the house before concentrating on the outside. A police photographer was still taking pictures of the kitchen, where the coffee-pot had fallen, spewing streams of black coffee onto the stove and floor. The telephone rang incessantly. To every call the policeman answering said, "The Chief will have a statement later."

The policeman at the phone came over to the table. "That was the A.P.," he said. "The wire services have gotten hold of this. We'll be mobbed in an hour."

The wire services. Ray remembered the haunted look that had only gradually left Nancy's face. He thought of the picture in this morning's paper, with her hand up as though trying to fend off blows. He pushed past Chief Coffin and hurried upstairs, opening the door of the master bedroom. The doctor was sitting next to Nancy, holding her hands. "You can hear me, Nancy," he was saying. "You know you can hear me. Ray is here. He's very worried about you. Talk to him, Nancy."

Her eyes were closed. Dorothy had helped Ray strip off the wet clothes. They'd put a fluffy yellow robe on her, but she seemed curiously small and inert inside it—not unlike a child herself.

Ray bent over her. "Honey, please, you've got to help the children. We've got to find them. They need you. Try, Nancy—please try."

"Ray, I wouldn't," Dr. Smathers warned. His lined, sensitive face was deeply creased. "She's had some kind of terrible shock—whether it was reading the article or something else. Her mind is fighting confronting it."

"But we've got to know what it was," Ray said intently. "Maybe she even saw someone take the children away. Nancy, I know. I understand. It's all right about the newspaper. We'll face that together. But, darling, where are the children? You must help us find them. Do you think they went near the lake?"

Nancy shuddered. A strangled cry came from somewhere in her throat. Her lips formed words: "Find them . . . find them."

"We will find them. But you must help, please. Honey, I'm going to help you sit up. You can. Now, come on."

Ray leaned down and supported her in his arms. He saw the raw skin on her face where the sand had burned it. There was wet sand still clinging to her hair. Why? Unless. . . .

"I gave her a shot," the doctor said. "It should relieve the anxiety, but it won't be enough to knock her out."

She felt so heavy and vague. This was the way she'd felt for such a long time—from the night Mother died . . . or maybe even before that—so defenseless, so pliable . . . so without ability to choose or move or even speak. She could remember how so many nights her eyes would be glued together—so heavy, so weary. Carl had been so patient with her. He had done everything for her. She had always told herself that she had to get stronger, had to overcome that terrible lethargy, but she never could.

But that was so long ago. She didn't think about that anymore—not about Carl; not about the children; not about Rob Legler, the handsome student who'd seemed to like her, who made her laugh. The children had been so gay when he was there, so happy. She had thought he was a real friend—but then he sat on the witness stand and said, "She told me that her children would be smothered. That was exactly what she said, four days before they disappeared."

"Nancy. Please. Nancy. Why did you go to the lake?"

She heard the stifled sound she made. The lake. Did the children go there? She must search for them.

She felt Ray lifting her and slumped against him, but then forced her body to begin to sit up. It would be so much easier to slip away, to slide into sleep just as she used to do.

"That's it. That's right, Nancy." Ray looked at the doctor. "Do you think a cup of coffee . . . ?"

The doctor nodded. "I'll ask Dorothy to make it."

Coffee. She'd been making coffee when she saw that picture in the paper. Nancy opened her eyes. "Ray," she whispered, "they'll know. Everyone will know. You can't hide . . . you can't hide." But there was something else. "The children." She clutched his arm. "Ray, find them—find my babies."

"Steady, honey. That's where we need you. You've got to tell us. Every single thing. Just get your bearing for a few minutes."

Dorothy came in with a cup of steaming coffee in her hand. "I made the instant. How is she?"

"She's coming round."

"Captain Coffin is anxious to begin questioning her."

"Ray!" Panic made Nancy clutch Ray's arm.

"Darling, it's just that we have to have help finding the children. It's all right."

She gulped the coffee, welcoming the searing, hot taste as she swallowed it. If she could just think . . . just wake up . . . just lose this terrible sleepiness.

Her voice. She could talk now. Her lips felt rubbery, thick, spongelike. But she had to talk . . . make them find the children. She wanted to go downstairs. She mustn't stay here . . . like last time . . . waiting in her room . . . unable to go downstairs . . . to see all the people downstairs . . . the policemen . . . the faculty wives. . . . Are there any relatives? . . . Do you want us to call anyone? . . . No one . . . no one . . . no one . . .

Leaning heavily on Ray's arm, she stood up unsteadily. Ray. She had his arm to lean on now. His children. His children.

"Ray . . . I didn't hurt them. . . ."

"Of course not, darling."

The voice too soothing . . . the shocked sound. Of course he was shocked. He was wondering why she would deny it. No good mother spoke of hurting her children. Why then did she . . . ?

With a supreme effort she groped toward the door. His arm around her waist steadied her steps. She couldn't feel her feet. They weren't there. She wasn't there. It was one of the nightmares. In a few minutes she'd wake up, as she had so many nights, and slip out of bed and go in to see Missy and Michael and cover them and then get back into bed—softly, quietly, not waking Ray. But in sleep he'd reach out and his arms would pull her close, and against the warm scent of him she'd be calmed and sleep.

They started down the stairs. So many policemen. Everybody looking up . . . curiously still . . . suspended in time.

Chief Coffin was at the dining-room table. She could feel his hostility. . . . It was like last time.

"Mrs. Eldredge, how do you feel?"

A perfunctory question, noncaring. Probably he wouldn't have bothered to ask except that Ray was there.

"I'm all right." She had never liked this man.

"We're searching for the children. I have every confidence that we'll find them quickly. But you must help us. When did you last see the children?"

"A few minutes before ten. I put them outside to play and went upstairs to make the beds."

"How long were you upstairs?"

"Ten minutes . . . not more than fifteen."

"Then what did you do?"

"I came downstairs. I was going to turn on a wash and call the children. But after I started the wash, I decided to heat the coffee. Then I saw the boy deliver the community paper."

"Did you speak to him?"

"No. I don't mean I saw him. I went to get the paper and he was just going around the corner."

"I see. What happened then?"

"I went back into the kitchen. I turned on the coffeepot—it was still quite warm. I started turning the pages of the paper."

"And you saw the article about yourself."

Nancy stared straight ahead and nodded her head.

"How did you react to seeing that article?"

"I think I started to scream . . . I don't know. . . ."

"What happened to the coffeepot?"

"I knocked it over. . . . The coffee went all over. It burned my hand."

"Why did you do that?"

"I don't know. I didn't mean to. It was just that I was going to burst. I knew that everyone would start looking at me again. They'd stare and whisper. They'd say I killed the children. And Michael mustn't ever see that. I ran with the paper. I pushed it into the fireplace. I lit a match and it burned . . . it started to burn . . . and I knew I had to get Michael and Missy—I had to hide them. But it was the way it was last time. When the children were gone. I ran out to get Michael and Missy. I was afraid."

"Now, this is important. Did you see the children?"

"No. They were gone. I started calling. I ran to the lake."

"Mrs. Eldredge, this is very important: Why did you go to the lake? Your husband tells me the children have never once been disobedient about going there. Why didn't you look on the road for them, or in the woods, or see if they'd decided to walk into town to buy you a birthday present? Why the lake?"

"Because I was afraid. Because Peter and Lisa were drowned. Because I had to find Michael and Missy. Missy's mitten was caught on the swing. She's always losing a mitten. I ran to the lake. I had to get the children. It's going to be just like last time . . . their faces all wet and quiet . . . and they won't talk to me. . . ."

Chief Coffin straightened up. His tone became formal. "Mrs. Eldredge," he said, "it is my duty to inform you that you have a right to legal advice before you answer any further questions and that anything you say can be used against you."

Without waiting for her response, he got up and stalked out of the room and to the back door. A car with a policeman at the wheel was waiting for him in the rear driveway. As he stepped from the house, thin, driving pellets of sleet stung his face and head. He got into the car and the wind blew the door closed behind him, scraping it against his shoe. He winced at the short stab of pain in his ankle and growled, "The lake."

Fat chance they had of doing any searching if this weather got any worse. At noon it was already so dark you'd think it was nighttime. The diving operation was a mess under optimal conditions. Maushop was among the biggest lakes on the Cape and one of the deepest and most treacherous. That was why over the years there'd been so many drownings there. You could be wading up to your waist and at the next step be in forty feet of water. If those kids had been drowned, it might be spring before their bodies surfaced. The way the temperature was dropping, the lake would be fit for ice skating in a few days.

The lakeside, normally deserted at this time of the year and certainly in this kind of weather, was crowded with bystanders, who huddled together in small clusters, silently watching the roped-off area where the divers and their apparatus were flanked by police.

Chief Coffin jumped out of the squad car and hurried to the beach. He went directly to Pete Regan, the lieutenant who was supervising the operation. Pete's eloquent shrug answered his unasked question.

Hunching his shoulders inside his coat, the Chief stamped his feet as the sleet melted into his shoes. He wondered if this was the spot from which Nancy Eldredge had dragged her kids into the water. Now men were risking their own lives because of her. God only knew where or when those poor little kids would be found. Shows what happens . . . A technicality . . . a convicted murderess gets off because a smart-ass lawyer gets a couple of bleeding-heart judges to declare a mistrial.

Angrily, he spat out Pete's name.

Pete turned to him quickly. "Sir?"

"How long are those guys planning to keep diving?"

"They've been down twice, and after this session, they'll try once more, then take a break and set up in a different location." He pointed to the television equipment. "Looks like we'll make the headlines tonight. You'd better have a statement ready."

With numbed fingers, the Chief dug into his coat pocket. "I've scribbled one down." He read it quickly. "We are conducting a massive effort to find the Eldredge children. Volunteers are making a block-by-block search of the immediate vicinity of her home as well as the neighboring wooded areas. Helicopters are conducting an air reconnaissance. The search of Maushop Lake, because of its proximity to the Eldredge home must be considered a normal extension of the investigation."

But a few minutes later, when he delivered that statement to the growing assemblage of reporters, one of them asked, "Is it true that Nancy Eldredge was found hysterical and drenched in this area of Maushop Lake this morning after her children disappeared?"

"That is true."

A thin, sharp-eyed reporter who he knew was connected with Boston Channel 5's news team asked, "In view of that fact and her past history, doesn't the search of the lake take on a new aspect?"

"We are exploring all possibilities."

Now the questions came thick and fast, the reporters interrupting one another to ask them. "In view of the past tragedy, wouldn't the disappearance of the Eldredge children be considered of suspicious origin?"

"To answer that question could prejudice Mrs. Eldredge's rights."

"When will you question her again?"

"As soon as possible."

"Is it known whether Mrs. Eldredge was aware of the article about her that came out this morning?"

"I believe she was."

"What was her reaction to that article?"

"I can't say."

"Isn't it a fact that most if not all of the people in this town were unaware of Mrs. Eldredge's past?"

"That is true."

"Were you aware of her identity?"

"No. I was not." The Chief spoke through clenched teeth. "No more questions."

Then, before he could get away, another question came. A reporter from the *Boston Herald* blocked his path. All the other news personnel stopped trying to get the Chief's attention when they heard him ask loudly, "Sir, in the past six years haven't there been several unsolved deaths of young children both on the Cape and on the nearby mainland?"

"That is true."

"Chief Coffin, how long has Nancy Harmon Eldredge been living on the Cape?"

"Six years, I believe."

"Thank you, Chief."

11

Jonathan Knowles did not realize how much time was slipping by. Neither was he aware of the activity in the area near Maushop Lake. His subconscious had registered the fact that heavier-than-usual traffic was passing on the road in front of his house. But his study was to the back of the house, and much of the sound was filtered out before it came to his ears.

After the first shock of realizing that Ray Eldredge's wife was the notorious Nancy Harmon, he'd gotten another cup of coffee and settled down at his desk. He resolved to stick to his schedule—to begin to study the Harmon murder case just as he'd planned. If he found that knowing Nancy Harmon personally in some way clouded his ability to write about her, he'd simply eliminate this chapter from his book.

He began his research by carefully studying the sensational article in the Cape paper. With grim detail that insidiously evoked horror in the reader, it reviewed Nancy Harmon's background as the young wife of a college professor . . . two children . . . a home on the college campus. An ideal situation until the day Professor Harmon sent a student to his house to repair the oil burner. The student was good-looking, glib and experienced with women. And Nancy—barely twenty-five herself—had flipped over him.

Jonathan read excerpts from the trial testimony in the article.

The student, Rob Legler, explained how he had met Nancy. "When Professor Harmon got that call from his wife about the oil burner not working, I was in his office. There's just nothing mechanical I can't fix, so I volunteered to go over. He didn't want me to do it, but he couldn't get the regular maintenance service and had to get the heat back on in his house."

"Did he give you any specific instructions concerning his family?" a district attorney asked.

"Yes. He said that his wife wasn't well and I shouldn't bother her; that if I needed anything, or wanted to discuss whatever problem I found, I should call him."

"Did you follow Professor Harmon's instructions?"

"I would have, sir, but I couldn't help the fact that his wife followed me around like a little dog."

"Objection! Objection!" But the defense attorney had been too late. The point had been made. And further evidence from the student had been totally damaging. He was asked if he had had any physical contact with Mrs. Harmon.

His answer was direct. "Yes, sir."

"How did it happen?"

"I was showing her where the emergency switch was on the oil burner. It was one of those old-fashioned hot-air-blower types, and the switch had caused the problem."

"Didn't Professor Harmon tell you not to trouble Mrs. Harmon with any questions or explanations?"

"She insisted on knowing about it. Said she had to learn how to manage things in her house. So I showed her. Then she was sort of leaning over me to try the switch, and . . . well, I figured, why not? . . . so I made a pass."

"What did Mrs. Harmon do?"

"She liked it. I could tell."

"Will you please explain exactly what happened?"

"It wasn't really what happened. 'Cause nothing much actually happened. It was just that she liked it. I sort of spun her around and grabbed her and kissed her—and after a minute she pulled away, but she didn't want to."

"What happened then?"

"I said something about that being pretty good."

"What did Mrs. Harmon say?"

"She just looked at me and said . . . almost like she wasn't talking to me . . . she said, 'I've got to get away.'"

"I figured I didn't want to get in any trouble. I mean, I didn't want to do anything to get kicked out of school and end up being drafted. That was the whole reason for the college scene. So I said, 'Look, Mrs. Harmon' . . . only then I decided it was about time to call her Nancy . . . so I said, 'Look, Nancy, this doesn't have to be a problem. We can work something out so we can get together without anyone ever guessing. You can't leave here—you've got the kids.'"

"How did Mrs. Harmon respond to that statement?"

"Well, it's funny. Just then the boy . . . Peter . . . came down the stairs looking for her. He was a real quiet kid—didn't say 'Boo.' She looked mad and said, 'The children'; then she sort of laughed and said, 'But they're going to be smothered.'"

"Mr. Legler, this is a crucial sentence you're quoting. Are you sure you are repeating Mrs. Harmon's exact phrasing?"

"Yes, sir, I am. It really made me feel spooky right then. That's why I'm so sure of it. But of course you don't really believe that anyone means it when they say something like that."

"On what date did Nancy Harmon make that statement?"

"It was on November thirteenth. I know because when I went back to school, Professor Harmon insisted on giving me a check for fixing the burner."

"November thirteenth . . . and four days later the Harmon children disappeared from their mother's automobile and eventually were washed in on the shores of San Francisco Bay with plastic bags over their heads—in effect, smothered."

"That's right."

The defense attorney had tried to reduce the impact of the story. "Did you continue to embrace Mrs. Harmon?"

"No. She went upstairs with the kids."

"Then we have only your statement that she enjoyed the kiss you forced on her."

"Believe me, I can tell a receptive babe when I'm with one."

And Nancy's sworn testimony when asked about that incident: "Yes, he did kiss me. Yes, I believe that I knew he was going to and I let him."

"Do you also remember making the statement that your children were going to be smothered?"

"Yes, I do."

"What did you mean by that statement?"

According to the article, Nancy simply looked past her attorney and stared unseeingly over the faces in the courtroom. "I don't know," she said in a dreamy voice.

Jonathan shook his head and swore silently. That girl should never have been permitted to take the witness stand. She did nothing except damage her own case. He continued reading and winced as he came to the description of the finding of those pathetic children. Washed in, both of them, two weeks and fifty miles apart. Bodies badly swollen, seaweed clinging to them, the little girl's body savagely mutilated—probably by shark bites; the handmade bright red sweaters with the white design still miraculously colorful against the small bodies.

After he'd finished reading the article, Jonathan turned his attention to the voluminous file Kevin had sent him. Leaning back in his chair, he began to read through it, starting with the first newspaper clipping headlining the disappearance of the Harmon children from their mother's automobile while she was shopping. Blowups of fuzzy snapshots of both of the children; a minutely detailed description of their weight and size and what they were wearing; anyone with any information please call this special number. With his carefully trained mind and eyes, Jonathan read rapidly, assorting and assimilating information, lightly underlining cogent facts he wanted to refer to later. When he began reading the transcript of the trial, he understood why Kevin had referred to Nancy Harmon as a sitting duck for the prosecutor. The girl didn't even make sense. She had played so completely into the prosecutor's hands the way she testified—without fight; her protestations of innocence sounding perfunctory and emotionless.

What had been the matter with her? Jonathan wondered. It was almost as though she didn't want to get off. At one point she'd even said to the husband right from the witness stand, "Oh, Carl, can you forgive me?"

The creases along Jonathan's forehead deepened as he recalled that just a few hours before he'd passed the Eldredges' house and glanced in at that young family around the breakfast table. He'd compared them with his own solitary state and had been envious. Now their life was ripped apart. They'd never be able to stay in as insular a community as the Cape, knowing that everywhere they went people were pointing and talking. Anyone would instantly recognize Nancy from that one picture. Even he remembered her wearing that tweed suit—and recently, too.

Suddenly Jonathan recalled the occasion. It had been at Lowery's Market. He'd run into Nancy when they were both shopping and they'd stopped for a few minutes to talk. He'd admired the suit, telling her that there was nothing better-looking than a good tweed—and pure wool, of course; none of that synthetic junk that had no depth or sheen.

Nancy had looked very pretty. A yellow scarf knotted casually at her neck had picked up the glint of yellow in the predominantly brown and rust-colored material. She'd smiled—a warm, lovely smile that wrapped you in it. The children were with her—nice, polite children, both of them. Then the boy had said, "Oh, Mommy, I'll get the cereal," and as he reached for it, he knocked over a pyramid of soup cans.

The clatter had brought everyone in the store running, including Lowery himself, who was a sour, disagreeable man. Many young mothers might have been embarrassed and started berating the child. Jonathan had admired the way Nancy said very quietly, "We're sorry, Mr. Lowery. It was an accident. We'll take care of it."

Then she said to the little boy, who looked stricken and worried, "Don't be upset, Mike. You didn't mean it. Come on. Let's pile them back up."

Jonathan had helped with the restacking, after first shooting a menacing glare at Lowery, who'd obviously been about to make some kind of remark. It seemed so hard to believe that seven years ago today that same considerate young woman could have deliberately taken the life of two other children—children she had brought into life.

But passion was a powerful motive, and she had been young. Maybe her very indifference at her trial had been acceptance of guilt, even though she couldn't publicly bring herself to admit such a heinous crime. He'd seen that kind of thing happen too.

The doorbell rang. Jonathan got up from his chair, surprised. Few people visited unannounced at the Cape, and any door-to-door selling was absolutely forbidden.

As he walked to the door Jonathan realized how stiff he'd become from sitting. To his amazement, his visitor was a policeman, a young man whose face he only vaguely recognized from seeing him in a squad car. *Selling some kind of tickets* was Jonathan's immediate thought, but he discarded that idea at once. The young officer accepted his invitation to step inside. There was something crisply efficient and serious about his demeanor. "Sir, I'm sorry to bother you but we're investigating the disappearance of the Eldredge children."

Then, while Jonathan stared at him, he pulled out a notebook. His eyes darting around the orderly house, he began his questions. "You live alone here, sir, do you not?"

Without answering, Jonathan reached past him and opened the massive front door. At last he became aware of the presence of cars driving down the road toward the lake and the sight of grim-faced men in heavy rain gear swarming through the neighborhood.

12

"Just sip this, Nancy. Your hands are so cold. It will help you. You need your strength." Dorothy's voice was cajoling. Nancy shook her head. Dorothy set the cup on the table, hoping the aroma of the fresh vegetables, bubbling in a spicy base of tomato soup, might tempt her.

"I made that yesterday," Nancy said tonelessly, "for the children's lunch. The children must be hungry."

Ray was sitting next to her, his arm slung protectively across the back of her chair, an ashtray filled high with ground-out cigarettes in front of him.

"Don't torture yourself, dear," he said quietly.

Outside, over the rattling of the shutters and windowpanes, they could hear the staccato sound of helicopters flying low.

Ray answered the question he saw on Nancy's face. "They've got three helicopters scanning the area. They'll spot the kids if they just wandered away. They've got volunteers from every town on the Cape. There are two planes over the bay and sound. Everyone's helping."

"And there are divers in the lake," Nancy said, "looking for my children's bodies." Her voice was a remote monotone.

After giving the statement to the news media, Chief Coffin had gone back to the police station to make a series of phone calls.

When they were completed, he returned to the Eldredge house, coming in just in time to hear Nancy's words. His practiced glance took in the staring quality of her eyes, the ominous stillness of her hands and body, the facile expression and voice. Approaching a state of shock again, and they'd be lucky if she was able to answer to her own name before long.

He looked past her, his eyes seeking Bernie Mills, the policeman he'd left on duty in the house. Bernie was standing at the doorway of the kitchen, poised to pick up the telephone if it rang. Bernie's sandy hair was plastered neatly over his bony skull. His prominent eyes, softened by short, blond lashes, moved horizontally. Accepting the signaled message, Chief Coffin looked again at the three people around the table. Ray got up, walked behind his wife's chair and put his hands on her shoulders.

Twenty years disappeared for Jed Coffin. He remembered the night he'd gotten a call at the precinct house when he was a rookie cop in Boston that Delia's folks had been in an accident and it wasn't likely they'd make it.

He'd gone home. She'd been sitting in the kitchen in her nightgown and robe, sipping a cup of her favorite instant hot chocolate, reading the paper. She'd turned, surprised to see him early but smiling, and before he said one word, he'd done just what Ray Eldredge was doing now—pressed his hands on her shoulders, holding her.

Hell, wasn't that the guts of the departure speech stewardesses used to rattle off on airplanes? "In the event of an emergency landing, sit straight, grip the arms of your seats, plant your feet solidly on the floor." What they were saying was "Let the shock pass through you."

"Ray, can I see you privately?" he asked brusquely.

Ray's hands continued to steady Nancy's shoulders as her body began to shake. "Did you find my children?" she asked. Now her voice was almost a whisper.

"Honey, he'd tell us if he found the kids. Just sit tight here. I'll be right back." Ray bent down and for an instant laid his cheek on hers. Without seeming to expect a response, he straightened up and led the Chief through the connecting foyer into the large living room.

Jed Coffin felt an unwilling admiration for the tall young man who positioned himself by the fireplace before turning to face him. There was something so gut-level self-possessed about Ray even in these circumstances. Fleetingly he remembered that Ray had been decorated for outstanding leadership under fire in Vietnam and given a field promotion to captain.

He had class, no doubt about that. There was class inherent in the way Ray stood and talked and dressed and moved; in the firm contours of his chin and mouth; in the strong, well-shaped hand that rested lightly on the mantel.

Stalling to regain his sense of rightness and authority, Jed looked slowly around the room. The wide oak floorboards shone softly under oval hooked rugs; a dry sink stood between the leaded paned windows. The mellow, creamy walls were covered with paintings. Jed realized that the scenes in them were familiar. The large painting over the fireplace was Nancy Eldredge's rock garden. The country-graveyard scene over the piano was that old private cemetery down the road from Our Lady of the Cape Church. The pine-framed painting over the couch had caught the homecoming flavor of Sesuit Harbor at sundown as all the boats came sailing in. The watercolor of the windswept cranberry bog had the old Hunt house—The Lookout—barely outlined in the background.

Jed had occasionally noticed Nancy Eldredge sketching around town, but never dreamed that she was any good. Most women he knew who fooled around with that sort of thing usually ended up framing stuff that looked like exhibits from Show and Tell.

Built-in bookcases lined the fireplace. The tables made of heavy old distressed pine weren't unlike the ones he remembered they'd donated to the church bazaar after his grandmother died. Pewter lamps like hers were on the low tables next to comfortable over-stuffed chairs. The rocker by the fireplace had a hand-embroidered cushion and back.

Somewhat uncomfortably, Jed compared this room with his own newly decorated living room. Delia had picked out black vinyl for the couch and chairs; a glass-topped table with steel legs; wall-to-wall carpeting—thick yellow shag that clawed at the shoes and faithfully preserved and displayed every drop of saliva or pee their still-untrained dachshund bestowed on it.

"What do you want, Chief?" Ray's voice was cold and un-friendly. The Chief knew that to Ray he was an enemy. Ray had seen through his routine admonition to Nancy about her rights. Ray knew exactly how he felt and was fighting him. Well if a fight was what he wanted . . .

With the ease born of experience garnered from countless simi-lar sessions, Jed Coffin sought out the weakness and directed his attention to it. "Who is your wife's lawyer, Ray?" he asked curtly.

A flicker of uncertainty, a stiffening of the body betrayed the answer. Just as Jed had figured, Ray hadn't taken the decisive step. Still trying to pretend his wife was the average distraught mother of missing children. Christ, he'd probably want to put her on a televi-sion news show tonight, handkerchief twisting in her hands, eyes swollen, voice pleading, "Give me back my children."

Well, Jed had news for Ray. His precious wife had done that scene before. Jed could get copies of the seven-year-old film the newspapers had called "a moving plea." In fact, the assistant dis-trict attorney in San Francisco had offered to provide it during their telephone conversation only half an hour ago. "It'll save that bitch the trouble of going through her act again," he'd said.

Ray was speaking quietly, his tone a hell of a lot more subdued. "We haven't contacted a lawyer," he said. "I hoped that maybe . . . with everyone searching . . ."

"Most of that search is going to be suspended pretty soon," Jed said flatly. "With this weather, there isn't going to be anyone able to see anything. But I've got to take your wife down to the station for questioning. And if you haven't arranged for a lawyer yet, I'll have the court appoint one for her."

"You can't do that!" Ray snapped the words furiously, then made an obvious effort to control himself. "What I mean is that you would destroy Nancy if you took her to a police-station setting. For years she used to have nightmares, and they were always the same: that she was in a police station being questioned and then that she was taken down a long corridor to the mortuary and made to identify her children. My God, man, she's in shock right now. Are you trying to make sure that she won't be able to tell us anything she may have seen?"

"Ray, my job is to get your children back."

"Yes, but you see what just reading that cursed article has done to her. And what about the bastard who wrote that article? Anyone vile enough to dig up that story and send it out might be capable of taking the children."

"Naturally we're working on that. That feature is always signed with a fictitious staff name, but the articles are actually free-lance submissions that if accepted involve a twenty-five-dollar payment."

"Well, who is the writer, then?"

"That was what we tried to find out," Jed replied. He sounded angry. "The covering letter instructed that the story was offered only on condition that if accepted, it would not be changed at all, that all the accompanying pictures would be used and that it would be published on November seventeenth—today. The editor told me that he found the story both well written and fascinating. In fact, he felt it was so good that he thought the writer was a fool to have submitted it to him for a lousy twenty-five dollars. But of course, he didn't say so. He dictated a letter accepting the conditions and enclosing the check."

Jed reached into his hip pocket for his notebook and flipped it open. "The letter of acceptance was dated October twenty-eighth. On the twenty-ninth the editor's secretary remembers receiving a phone call asking if a decision had been reached about the Harmon article. It was a bad connection and the voice was so muffled she could hardly hear the caller, but she told him—or her—that a check was in the mail, care of General Delivery, Hyannis Port. The check was made out to one J. R. Penrose. The next day it was picked up."

"Man or woman?" Ray asked quickly.

"We don't know. As you have to realize, a town like Hyannis Port has a fair number of tourists going through it even at this time of the year. Anyone requesting something from General Delivery would only have to ask for it. No clerk seems to remember the letter, and so far the twenty-five-dollar check hasn't been cashed. We can work our way back to J. R. Penrose when it is. Frankly, it wouldn't surprise me if the writer turns out to be one of our own little old ladies in town. They can be just wonderful at digging into gossip."

Ray stared into the fireplace. "It's cool in here," he said. "A fire will feel good." His eye fell on the cameos on the mantelpiece that Nancy had painted of Michael and Missy when they were babies. He swallowed over the stinging lump that suddenly closed his throat.

"I don't think you really need a fire in here now, Ray," Jed said quietly. "I asked you to step in here because I want you to tell Nancy to get dressed and come with us to the station house."

"No . . . no . . . please . . ." Chief Coffin and Ray whirled to face the archway leading into the room. Nancy was standing there, one hand leaning against the carved oak archway for support. Her hair had dried, and she had pulled it into a bun caught loosely against the nape of her neck. The strain of the past hours had turned her skin a chalky white that was accentuated by the dark hair. An almost detached expression was settling into her eyes.

Dorothy was behind her. "She wanted to come in." Dorothy's voice was apologetic.

Now she felt the accusation in Ray's eyes as he hurried over to them. "Ray, I'm sorry. I couldn't make her stay inside."

Ray pulled Nancy against him. "It's all right, Dorothy," he said briefly. His voice changed and became tender. "Honey, just relax. Nobody's going to hurt you."

Dorothy felt the dismissal in his tone. He had counted on her to keep Nancy away while he spoke to the Chief, and she couldn't even do that much. She was useless here — useless. "Ray," she said stiffly. "It's ridiculous to bother you about this, but the office just phoned to remind me that Mr. Kragopoulos, who wrote about the Hunt property, wants to see it at two o'clock. Shall I get someone else to take him up there?"

Ray looked over Nancy's head as he held her firmly against him. "I don't give a damn," he snapped. Then quickly he said, "I'm sorry, Dorothy. I would appreciate it if you showed the place; you know The Lookout and can sell it if there's real interest. Poor old Mr. Hunt needs the money."

"I haven't told Mr. Parrish that we might be bringing people in today."

"His lease clearly states that we have the right to show the house at any time with simply a half hour's telephone notice. That's why he has it so cheap. Give him a call from the office and tell him you're coming."

"All right." Uncertainly, Dorothy waited, not wanting to go. "Ray . . ."

He looked at her, understanding her unspoken wish but dismissing her. "There's nothing you can do here now, Dorothy. Come back when you've finished at The Lookout."

She nodded and turned to go. She didn't want to leave them; she wanted to stay with them, sharing their anxiety. Ever since that first day when she'd walked into Ray's office, he'd been a lifeline for her. After nearly twenty-five years of planning her every activity with Kenneth or around Kenneth's schedule, she'd been so rootless and, for the first time in her life, frightened. But working with Ray, helping him to build the business, using her knowledge of interior decorating to spark people to buy the houses, then invest in renovating them had filled so much of the void. Ray was such a fair, fine person. He'd given her such a generous profit-sharing arrangement. She couldn't have thought more of him if he'd been her own son. When Nancy had come, she'd been so proud that Nancy trusted her. But there was a reserve in Nancy that didn't permit any real intimacy, and now she felt like an unnecessary bystander. Wordlessly she left them, got her coat and scarf and went to the back door.

She braced herself against the wind and sleet as she opened it. Her car was parked halfway around the semicircular back driveway. She was glad she didn't have to go through the front drive. One of the networks had a television van parked in front of the house.

As she hurried toward her car, she saw the swing on the tree at the edge of the property. That was where the children had been playing and where Nancy had found the mitten. How many times had she herself pushed the children on that swing? Michael and Missy . . . The awful possibility that something might have happened to them—that they might be dead—gave her a terrible choking sensation. *Oh, please not that . . . almighty and merciful God, please not that.* She'd joked once about being their surrogate grandmother, and then the look of pain had been so unmistakable on Nancy's face that she had wanted to bite her tongue off. It had been a presumptuous thing to say.

She stared at the swing, lost in thought, unmindful of the wet sleet stinging her face. Whenever Nancy stopped in the office, the children made a beeline for her desk. She tried to always have a surprise for them. Just yesterday when Nancy had come in with Missy, she'd had tollhouse cookies she'd baked the night before as the special treat. Nancy had been on her way to look at drapery material, and Dorothy had offered to mind Missy and pick up Michael at kindergarten. "It's hard to select material unless you can really concentrate," she'd said, "and I have to pick up some title-search papers at the courthouse. It will be fun to have company, and on the way back we'll get some ice cream, if that's all right." Only twenty-four hours ago. . . .

"Dorothy."

Startled, she looked up. Jonathan must have cut through the woods from his house. His face was deeply creased today. She knew he must be nearly sixty years old, and today he looked every bit of it. "I just heard about the Eldredge children," he said. "I've got to talk to Ray. Possibly I can help."

"That's nice of you," Dorothy said unsteadily. The concern in his voice was oddly comforting. "They're inside."

"No trace of the children yet?"

"No."

"I saw the article in the paper."

Belatedly, Dorothy realized that sympathy was not being offered to her. There was a coolness in Jonathan's tone, a reproof that clearly reminded her that she had lied to him about having known Nancy in Virginia. Wearily, she opened the door of her car. "I have an appointment," she said abruptly. Without giving him time to answer, she got in and started up the engine. It was only when her vision blurred that she realized that tears were swimming in her eyes.

13

The clatter of the helicopters pleased him. It reminded him of the last time, when everyone for miles around the University had fanned out looking for the children. He stared out the front window overlooking the bay. The gray water was caked with ice near the jetty. Earlier the radio had spoken of gale warnings and sleet or rain mixed with snow. For once, the weatherman had been right. The wind was whipping the bay into angry whitecaps. He watched as a flock of gulls flew unsteadily in a futile effort to make headway against the wind.

He carefully consulted the indoor-outdoor thermometer. Twenty-eight degrees out there now—a drop of twenty degrees since the morning. The helicopters and search planes wouldn't be up much longer in this. There wouldn't be many searchers out on land either.

High tide was seven o'clock tonight. At that time he'd take the children up through the attic to the outer balcony they called the widow's walk. The water at high tide covered the beach below, broke furiously against the retaining wall and then, sucked by the violent undertow, rolled back to sea. That would be the time to drop the children . . . over . . . down . . . They might not be washed in for weeks. . . . But even if they were found in a few days, he'd prepared for that. He'd given them only milk and cookies. He wouldn't be fool enough to feed them anything that would suggest that a person other than Nancy had fed them a real meal after breakfast. Of course, hopefully they'd be beyond analysis when they were found.

He chuckled. In the meantime, he had five hours: five long hours to look at the floodlights that were being set up near Nancy's house and the lake; five hours to be with the children. Even the boy, come to think of it, was a beautiful child . . . such soft skin, and that perfectly formed body.

But it was the little girl. She looked so much like Nancy . . . that silky, beautiful hair and small, well-formed ears. He turned from the window abruptly. The children were lying together on the couch. The sedative he'd put in the milk had both of them sleeping. The boy's arm was protectively over his sister. But he didn't even stir when he picked up the little girl. He'd just take her inside and put her on the bed and undress her. She made no sound as he carefully carried her into the bedroom and laid her down. He went into the bathroom and turned on the faucets in the tub, testing the gushing water until it reached the temperature he wanted. When the tub was filled, he tested the water again with his elbow. A little hotter than it should be, but that was all right. It would cool in a few minutes.

He sucked in his breath. He was wasting time. Swiftly he opened the door of the medicine cabinet and pulled out the can of baby powder he'd slipped into his coat pocket at Wiggins' Market this morning. As he was about to close the door, he noticed the little rubber duck poked back behind the shaving cream. He'd forgotten about that . . . why it had been used the last time . . . how appropriate. Laughing softly, he reached for the duck; ran it under cold water, feeling the lack of elasticity and the cracking of the rubber; then tossed it into the tub. It was a good idea to distract children sometimes.

Grabbing the can of powder, he hurried back into the bedroom.

Swiftly his fingers unbuttoned Missy's jacket and pulled it off. Easily, he slipped the turtleneck polo shirt over her head, bringing her undershirt with it. He sighed—a lingering, groaning sound—and picked up the little girl, hugging her limp body to him. Three years old. Just a beautiful age. She stirred and started to open her eyes. "Mommy, Mommy . . ." It was a weak, lazy cry—so dear, so precious.

The phone rang.

Angrily he tightened his grip on the child, and she began to wail—a hopeless, lethargic cry.

He'd let the phone ring. He never, never got calls. Why now? His eyes narrowed. It might be a call from the town, asking him to volunteer in the search. He'd better answer. It might be suspicious not to answer. He tossed Missy back onto the bed and closed the bedroom door securely before he picked up the phone in the sitting room. "Yes." He made his voice sound formal and cold.

"Mr. Parrish, I hope I haven't disturbed you. This is Dorothy Prentiss of Eldredge Realty. I'm sorry to give you such short notice, but I'll be bringing a prospective buyer for the house over in twenty minutes. Will you be there or shall I use my passkey to show your apartment?"

14

Lendon Miles turned right off Route 6A onto Paddock Path. All the way down on the trip from Boston he'd kept his radio at a news station, and most of the news was about Nancy Eldredge and the missing Eldredge children.

According to the bulletins, Maushop Lake had been divided into sections, but it would take divers at least three days to search it properly. Maushop Lake was filled with underwater ledges. Police Chief Coffin of Adams Port was quoted as explaining that at one point it was possible to walk halfway across the lake and still be in water only to the waist; a few yards away, only five feet from the shore, the water became forty feet deep. The underwater ledges caught and held objects and made the search hazardous and inconclusive. . . .

The bulletins announced that helicopters, small seaplanes and ground search parties had been out but gale warnings for the Cape were in effect and the air search was being called off.

At the news that Nancy Eldredge was expected to be taken to Police Headquarters for questioning, Lendon unconsciously accelerated the car. He felt a desperate urgency about getting to Nancy. But he quickly found that he had to reduce his speed. Sleet was glazing the windshield so rapidly that the defroster was having trouble melting the crusting ice.

When at last he turned into Paddock Path, he had no trouble finding the Eldredge home. There was no mistaking the center of activity on the street. Halfway up the road, a television van was parked across the street from a house that had two police cars stationed in front of it. Private cars lined the road near the television van. Many bore special press identifications.

The entrance to the semicircular driveway was blocked by one of the police cars. Lendon stopped and waited for a policeman to come over to him. When one did, his tone was brusque. "State your business, please."

Lendon had anticipated the question and was ready. He handed out his card with a note scrawled on it. "Please take this to Mrs. Eldredge."

The policeman looked uncertain. "If you'll wait here, Doctor . . . I'll have to check." He returned promptly, his attitude subtly less hostile. "I'll move the squad car out of the way. Park in the driveway and go into the house, sir."

From across the street, reporters had been watching the byplay, and they hurried over. One of them thrust a microphone in front of Lendon's face as he got out of the car.

"Dr. Miles, may we ask you a few questions?"

Without waiting for an answer, he went on quickly, "Sir, you are a prominent psychiatrist on the staff of Harvard Medical School. Has the Eldredge family sent for you?"

"No one has sent for me," Lendon replied sharply. "I am a friend—was a friend—of Mrs. Eldredge's mother. I have come here because of personal friendship and that alone."

He tried to pass, but was blocked by the microphone-holding reporter. "You say you were a friend of Mrs. Eldredge's mother. Will you tell us this: Was Nancy Harmon Eldredge ever a patient of yours?"

"Absolutely not!" Lendon literally shoved his way through the reporters and onto the porch. The front door was being held open by another policeman. "Right in there," the man said, indicating the room to the right.

Nancy Eldredge was standing at the fireplace next to a tall young man, undoubtedly her husband. Lendon would have known her anywhere. The finely chiseled nose, the large midnight-blue eyes that looked straight out from under thick lashes, the widow's peak at the hairline, the profile that was so like Priscilla's . . .

Ignoring the openly hostile look of the police officer and the scrutiny of the craggy-faced man at the window, he went directly to Nancy. "I should have come before," he said.

The girl's eyes had a staring quality, but she knew what he meant. "I thought you would come last time," she told him — "when Mother died. I was so sure you would come. And you didn't."

Expertly, Lendon measured the symptoms of shock that he could see: the enlarged pupils; the rigidity of her body; the low, monotone quality of her voice. He turned to Ray. "I want to help if there's any possible way," he said.

Ray studied him intently and instinctively liked what he saw. "Then as a doctor, try to persuade the Chief here that it would be a disaster to take Nancy to the police station," he said flatly.

Nancy stared into Lendon's face. She felt so detached — as though each minute she were slipping farther and farther away. But there was something about this Dr. Miles. Mother had liked him so much; Mother's letters had sounded so happy; more and more often his name had been in them.

When her mother had come out to visit her at college she'd asked about the doctor; how important was he? But Carl was with them, and Mother didn't seem to want to talk about him then. She just smiled and said, "Oh, terribly important, but I'll fill you in later, dear."

She could remember that so clearly. She had wanted to meet

Dr. Miles. Somehow she'd been sure that when he heard about Mother's accident he would call her. She had needed to talk to someone who loved Mother too. . . .

"You loved my mother, didn't you?" It was her voice asking that question. She wasn't even aware that she had intended to ask it.

"Yes, I did. Very much. I didn't know that she had told you about me. I thought you might resent me. I should have tried to help you."

"Help me now!"

He took her hands in his, her terribly cold hands. "I'll try, Nancy, I promise." She sagged, and her husband put his arms around her.

Lendon liked the looks of Ray Eldredge. The younger man's face was gray with anxiety, but he bore himself well. His attitude toward his wife was protective. He obviously had a firm grip on his own emotions. Lendon noticed the small framed picture on the table next to the sofa. It was an outdoor snapshot of Ray holding a little boy and girl. . . . The missing children. Of course. What a handsome family. Interesting that nowhere in this room could he see a single picture of Nancy. He wondered if she ever allowed herself to be photographed.

"Nancy, come, honey. You've got to rest." Ray gently eased her down onto the sofa and lifted her feet. "Now, that's better." She obediently leaned back. Lendon watched as her eyes focused on the snapshot of Ray and the children and then closed in pain. A shiver made her entire body tremble.

"I think we'd better stir up this fire," he told Ray. He selected a medium-sized log from the basket on the fireplace and threw it onto the smoldering hearth. A shower of flames sprayed up.

Ray tucked a quilt around Nancy. "You're so cold, darling," he said. For an instant he held her face between his hands. Tears trickled from under her closed eyelids and dampened his fingers.

"Ray, have I your permission to represent Nancy as her legal counsel?" Jonathan's voice had subtly altered. It was infused with an authoritative crispness. Calmly he met the astonished stares. "I assure you I am well qualified," he said drily.

"Legal counsel," Nancy whispered. From somewhere she could see the colorless, frightened face of the lawyer last time. Domes, that had been his name—Joseph Domes. He'd kept saying to her, "But you must tell me the truth. You must trust me to help you." Even he hadn't believed her.

But Jonathan Knowles was different. She liked his bigness and the courtly way he always spoke to her, and he was so attentive to the children when he stopped to speak. . . . Lowery's Market—that was it. A couple of weeks ago, he'd helped her and Mike to stack up the cans that Mike had knocked over. He liked her, she was sure. Instinctively she knew it. She opened her eyes. "Please," she said, looking at Ray.

Ray nodded. "We'd be very grateful, Jonathan."

Jonathan turned to Lendon. "Doctor, may I have your medical opinion as to the advisability of allowing Mrs. Eldredge to be taken to the police station for questioning?"

"It is highly inadvisable," Lendon said promptly. "I would urge that any questioning be done here."

"But I can't remember." Nancy's voice was weary, as though she had said those same words too many times. "You say I know where my children are. But I don't remember anything from when I saw that paper in the kitchen this morning until I heard Ray calling me." She looked up at Lendon, her eyes clouded and staring. "Can you help me to remember? Is there any way?"

"What do you mean?" Lendon asked.

"I mean isn't there some way you can give me something so that if I know . . . or saw . . . or did . . . Even if I did something . . . I have to know . . . That isn't something you can hide. If there is some awful part of me that could hurt my children . . . we have to know that too. And if there isn't but if somehow I know where they might be, we're just wasting time now."

"Nancy, I won't let—" But Ray stopped when he saw the anguish in her face.

"Is it possible to help Nancy to remember what happened this morning, Doctor?" Jonathan asked.

"Perhaps. She is probably suffering from a form of amnesia which is not uncommon after what to her was a catastrophic experience. In medical terms, it's a hysterical amnesia. Under an injection of sodium amytal, she would be relaxed and probably able to tell us what happened—the truth as she knows it."

"Answers given under sedation would not be admissible in court," Jed snapped. "I can't have you questioning Mrs. Eldredge like that."

"I used to have such a good memory," Nancy murmured. "Once at college we had a contest to see who could recall what she'd done every day. You just kept going backwards day by day until you couldn't remember anymore. I won by so much that it was a joke in the dorm. Everything was so clear. . . ."

The telephone rang and had the effect of a pistol exploding in the room. Nancy shrank back, and Ray covered her hands with his. They all waited silently until the policeman on duty at the phone came into the room. He said, "Long distance for you, Chief."

"I can assure you that this is the call I've been trying to place," Jed told Nancy and Ray. "Mr. Knowles, I'd appreciate it if you'd come with me. You too, Ray."

"Be right back, darling," Ray murmured to Nancy. Then he looked into Lendon's face. Satisfied with what he saw, he followed the other men out of the room.

Lendon watched as relief drained from Nancy's expression. "Every time it rings, I think somebody has found the children and they're safe," she murmured. "And then I think it will be like last time . . . when the call came."

"Steady," Lendon said. "Nancy, this is important. Tell me when you started having trouble remembering specific events."

"When Peter and Lisa died . . . but maybe even before that. It's so hard to remember the years I was married to Carl."

"That could be because you associate those years with the children and it's too painful to remember anything about them."

"But during those five years . . . I was so terribly tired so much . . . after Mother died . . . always so tired. Poor Carl . . . so patient. He did everything for me. He got up with the children at night—even when they were babies. Everything was such an effort for me. . . . After the children disappeared, I couldn't remember . . . like . . . like now . . . I just couldn't." Her voice had begun to rise.

Ray came back into the room. Something had happened. Lendon could see it in the taut lines around Ray's mouth, the slight trembling of his hands. He found himself praying: *Please, don't let it be bad news.*

"Doctor, could you speak with Jonathan for a minute, please?" Ray was making a determined effort to keep his voice even.

"Certainly." Lendon hurried toward the arched doorway that led into the family and dining room, sure that the phone call had badly upset Ray.

When he got to the dining room, Chief Coffin was still on the phone. He was barking orders to the lieutenant on duty at the station: "Get the hell down to that post office and round up every clerk who was on duty October thirtieth and don't stop questioning them until somebody remembers who picked up that letter from the *Community News* addressed to J. R. Penrose. I need a full description, and I need it now." He slammed the receiver into its cradle.

There was new tension in Jonathan too. Without preamble, he said, "Doctor, we can't lose any time in trying to break through Nancy's amnesia. To fill you in, I have a very complete file on the

Harmon case because of a book I'm writing. I've spent the last three hours studying that file and reading the article that appeared in today's paper. Something struck me that seemed of the greatest possible importance, and I asked Chief Coffin to phone the District Attorney in San Francisco and check my theory. His assistant has just returned the call."

Jonathan reached into his pocket for his pipe, clamped his teeth on it without lighting it and continued, "Doctor, as you may know, in cases of missing children where foul play is suspected, the police will often deliberately withhold a piece of information so that they have some help in sifting through the inevitable meaningless clues they receive after a publicized disappearance."

He began to speak more quickly, as though he felt he was letting too much time pass. "I noticed that all the newspaper accounts seven years ago described the missing children as wearing red cardigan sweaters with a white pattern when they disappeared. Nowhere in any of the extensive newspaper coverage is there an exact description of what that pattern was. I surmised—correctly—that the motif of the pattern had been deliberately withheld."

Jonathan looked directly at Lendon, wanting him to understand immediately the importance of what he was about to tell him. "The article which appeared in the *Cape Cod Community News* clearly states that when the Harmon children disappeared they were wearing red cardigan sweaters with an unusual white sailboat design, and that they were still wearing them when their bodies were washed ashore weeks later. Now, Nancy, of course, was aware of that sailboat design. She made those sweaters herself. But only one other person outside of the top people on the San Francisco investigative staff knew about that design." Jonathan's voice rose in pitch. "If we assume Nancy's innocence, that person was the one who kidnapped the Harmon children seven years ago—

and who one month ago wrote the story that appeared in today's paper!"

"Then you mean—" Lendon began.

"Doctor, I mean, as Nancy's lawyer and friend, if you can break through her amnesia, do it—quickly! I have persuaded Ray that it is worthwhile to waive any immunity. The overriding necessity is to find out what Nancy may know; otherwise it will surely be too late to help her children."

"Can I telephone a drugstore and get something delivered?" Lendon asked.

"You call, Doctor," Jed ordered. "I'll send a squad car over to pick up whatever you need. Here—I'll dial the drugstore for you."

Quietly Lendon phoned his instructions and when he had finished went into the kitchen for a glass of water. *Oh, the waste,* he thought—*the awful waste.* The tragedy that had begun with Priscilla's accident . . . cause and effect . . . cause and effect. If Priscilla had not died, she probably would have persuaded Nancy not to marry so young. The Harmon children would never have been born. Sharply he pulled himself back from useless speculation. The kitchen had obviously been gone over for fingerprints. Grains of powder were still evident on the countertops, around the sink and on the stove. No one had wiped up the stain from where coffee had spilled.

He returned to the dining room to hear Chief Coffin say, "Remember, Jonathan, I may well be exceeding my authority as it is. But I'm going to have a tape recorder on in that room when that girl is questioned. If she confesses to anything under sedation, we may not be able to use it directly, but I'll know what to ask her under regular questioning later."

"She's not going to confess to anything," Jonathan said impatiently. "What concerns me is that if we accept her innocence as a fact—not only about Michael and Missy's disappearance but also her innocence in the murder of the Harmon children—then our next supposition becomes this: if the killer of the Harmon children wrote the article for the *Community News* and used a Hyannis post office, he has been here on the Cape for some time."

"And you are saying that he abducted the Eldredge children this morning," Chief Coffin finished.

Jonathan relit his pipe and puffed at it vigorously before answering. "I'm afraid so," he said. His tone of voice, deliberately devoid of expression, made Lendon understand what he meant. Jonathan believed that if the killer of the Harmon children had taken Michael and Missy Eldredge, they were probably dead.

"On the other hand," Jed theorized, "if we remove Mrs. Eldredge as a suspect, it is equally possible that someone who never came forward at the Harmon trial knew something about those murders, wrote that article and has now kidnapped the Eldredge children. A third possibility is that the two cases are unrelated except that someone reading that article and recognizing Nancy Eldredge has become involved in the disappearance this morning. The children may have been taken by a frustrated mother who feels Nancy doesn't deserve them. I've seen a lot screwier rationalizations than that in my day."

"Jed," snapped Jonathan, "what I'm trying to say is that no matter who else may have become involved, one fact is very clear: I don't believe there's any question but that Nancy knew more than she told about the disappearance of her children seven years ago."

Lendon raised an eyebrow. Jed frowned deeply. At the expressions on the faces of the two men, Jonathan slapped his hand impatiently on the table. "I'm not saying that that girl is guilty. I am saying that she knew more than she told; probably knew more than she was aware of knowing. Look at the pictures of her on the witness stand. Her face is an absolute blank. Read the testimony.

For God's sake, man, read the trial testimony. That girl was out of it. Her lawyer may have upset her conviction on a technicality, but that doesn't mean that he didn't let that district attorney crucify her. That entire setup stank, and you're trying to reenact it here."

"I'm trying to get away from your theories . . . and that's all they are . . . and perform my job, which is to recover those children—dead or alive—and find out who abducted them." Jed was clearly out of patience. "In one breath you tell me she's too sick to be questioned and in the next one that she knows more than she ever let on. Look, Jonathan, you said yourself that writing a book about questionable verdicts is a hobby with you. But those lives aren't hobbies with me, and I'm not here to help you play chess with the law."

"Hold on." Lendon put a restraining hand on the Chief's arm. "Mr. Knowles . . . Jonathan . . . you believe that whatever knowledge Nancy has of the death of her first family may help us find the Eldredge children."

"Exactly. But the problem is to extract that knowledge, not drive it deeper into her subconscious. Dr. Miles, you are considered an expert in the use of sodium amytal in psychiatry, are you not?"

"Yes, I am."

"Is it possible you might be able to have Nancy reveal not only what she knows of this morning's events—which I suspect will be nothing—but also information about the past that she doesn't even know she has herself?"

"It's possible."

"Then unless she can tell us something tangible about Michael and Missy's whereabouts, I beg you to try."

When Dorothy was readmitted to the house an hour later, the family room and kitchen were deserted except for Bernie Miles, the policeman charged with answering the phones. "They're all in there," he said, jerking his head toward the front parlor. "Something pretty queer going on."

Dorothy hurried down the hall, but stopped at the doorway of the room. The greeting she was about to utter died on her lips as she took in the scene before her.

Nancy was lying on the couch, a pillow under her head, a quilt tucked around her. A stranger who looked like a doctor was sitting beside her, speaking softly. Nancy's eyes were closed. An anguished-looking Ray and grim-faced Jonathan were side by side on the love seat. Jed Coffin was sitting at a table behind the couch, holding a microphone pointed toward Nancy.

As Dorothy realized what was happening, she sank into a chair, not bothering to take off her coat. Numbly she slipped her chilled fingers into the deep side pockets, unconsciously gripping the scrap of damp, fuzzy wool that she felt in the right-hand pocket.

"How do you feel, Nancy? Are you comfortable?" Lendon's voice was tranquil.

"I'm afraid. . . ."

"Why?"

"The children . . . the children . . ."

"Nancy. Let's talk about this morning. Did you sleep well last night? When you woke up did you feel rested?"

Nancy's voice was reflective. "I dreamed. I dreamed a lot. . . ."

"What did you dream about?"

"Peter and Lisa. . . . They'd be so grown up. . . . They're dead seven years. . . ." She began to sob. Then, as Jonathan's iron grip held Ray back, she cried, "How could I have killed them? They were my children! How could I have killed them . . . ?"

15

B efore Dorothy had met John Kragopoulos at the office, she had tried to camouflage her red-rimmed eyes with a dusting powder. She'd tried to convince herself that after all, showing the Hunt place would be an outlet, an action that could be concentrated on for a little while and keep her mind from its endless squirreling for clues to the children's whereabouts. What clues?

Normally she took prospective clients on a brief tour of the area before showing a property, to let them see the beaches and lakes and marina; the stately old homes that were scattered between Cranberry Highway and the bay; the breathtaking view from Maushop Tower; the old town landmarks.

But today, with the sleet beating a sharp tattoo on the car roof and windows, with the sky filled with black fields of clouds and with the cold sea air chilling the very marrow of the bones, she headed directly for The Lookout.

It was so hard to keep her mind on what she was doing. She felt so distracted and shaken. She who hadn't cried in years was having to bite her lips to keep tears back. There was a crushing weight on her shoulders, a weight of grief and fear that she could not hope to support alone.

As she drove the car along the treacherously slick road, she stole an occasional glance at the swarthy-complexioned man beside her.

John Kragopoulos was somewhere in his mid forties. He had the build of a weight lifter, yet there was an innate courtliness in his bearing that complemented his slightly accented manner of speaking.

He told Dorothy that he and his wife had just sold their restaurant in New York and agreed their next venture would be in an area where they would want to settle permanently. They were anxious to be where well-to-do retired people could be found for winter business, as well as the summer resort trade.

Mentally reviewing these points, Dorothy said, "I'd never recommend investing in a restaurant over on the other side of the Cape anymore; it's just one mass of motels and pizza parlors now—absolutely frightful zoning—but this side of the Cape is still lovely. The Lookout has unlimited possibilities as a restaurant and inn. During the thirties it was renovated extensively and turned into a country club. People didn't have money to join expensive country clubs at that time, and so it never caught on. Eventually Mr. Hunt bought the house and grounds—nine acres in all, including one thousand feet of waterfront property and one of the finest views on the Cape."

"The Lookout was originally a captain's house, was it not?"

Dorothy realized that John Kragopoulos had done some homework on the place—a sure sign of real interest. "Yes, it was," she agreed. "It was built by a whaling captain in the sixteen-nineties as a gift for his bride. The most recent renovation, forty years ago, added two floors, but the original roof was put back on, including one of those charming little balconies near the peak of the chimney—widow's walks they're called, because so many of the captains' wives used to watch in vain for their men to come back from a voyage."

"The sea can be treacherous," her passenger agreed. "By the way, is there a dock with the property? If I relocate up here, I plan to buy a boat."

"A very good one," Dorothy assured him. "Oh, dear!" She gasped as the car skidded dangerously when she turned onto the narrow, winding road that led up to The Lookout. She managed to straighten the wheels and glanced anxiously at her passenger. But he seemed unperturbed, and remarked mildly that she was a brave lady to risk driving on such icy roads.

Like a surgeon's knife the words penetrated to the core of Dorothy's misery. It was a frightful day. It would be a miracle if the car didn't skid right off this narrow road. Whatever interest she had talked herself into about showing the house vanished. If the weather were only decent, the beaches and streets and woods would be filled with men and boys looking for Missy and Michael; but in this weather only the heartiest would think of going out—especially since many felt it was a useless search.

"I don't mind driving," she said thickly; "I'm just sorry Mr. Eldredge isn't with us. But I'm sure you understand."

"I understand very well," John Kragopoulos said. "What an agonizing experience for the parents to have young children missing! I am only sorry to take your time today. As a friend and coworker, you must be concerned."

Determinedly, Dorothy did not let herself reply to the sympathy in the man's voice and manner. "Let me tell you more about the house," she said. "All the windows to the front look over the water. The front door has an exquisite fan-light, which was a feature on the finer houses of that period. The large downstairs rooms have wonderful gable-end fireplaces. On a day like this many people would enjoy going to a restaurant where they can watch the storm while they enjoy a good drink and good food and a warm fire. Here we are."

They rounded the curve, and The Lookout was in full view. To Dorothy it seemed strangely bleak and dreary as it loomed against the shrouded embankment. The weather-beaten shingles were stark gray. The sleet slapping against the windows and porches seemed to reveal mercilessly the peeling shutters and sagging outside steps.

She was surprised to see that Mr. Parrish had left the garage doors open. Maybe he had been carrying groceries his last trip in and had forgotten to come out again to pull the door down. But it was a break for them. She'd drive right into the roomy garage and park her car beside his old station wagon, and they'd be able to make a run for the house with some protection from the garage overhang.

"I've got a key to the back door," she told John Kragopoulos after they'd gotten out of the car. "I'm so sorry I didn't think to bring Ray's golf umbrella. I hope you don't get too wet."

"Don't worry about me," he chided. "I'm pretty rugged. Don't I look it?"

She smiled faintly and nodded. "All right, let's make a dash for it." They ran out of the garage and kept close to the wall as they covered the fifty feet to the kitchen door. Even so, the sleet pelted their faces and the wind pulled at their coats.

To her annoyance, Dorothy found that the door was double-locked. Mr. Parrish might have been more considerate, she fumed. She rummaged through her bag for the key to the top lock and found it. She gave a quick yank at the bell to let Mr. Parrish know they had arrived. She could hear the ringing sound echoing upstairs as she pushed the door in.

Her prospective buyer seemed unperturbed as he brushed sleet from his coat and dried his face with a handkerchief. He was a low-keyed person, Dorothy decided. She had to will herself not to sound either nervous or overly talkative showing the place. Every fiber of her being made her want to rush this man through the house. *See this . . . and this . . . and this . . . Now let me go back to Ray and Nancy, please; maybe there's been some news of the children.*

She did notice that he was carefully studying the kitchen. Deliberately she reached for her own handkerchief to dab at her face, aware suddenly that she was wearing her new suede winter coat. This morning she'd decided to wear it because of this appointment. She knew it was becoming and that the gray shade complemented her pepper-and-salt-colored hair. The big deep pockets were what made her conscious that she wasn't wearing her old storm coat—but the storm coat would certainly have been a better choice today.

And there was something else. Oh, yes. When she had put on the coat, she had wondered if Jonathan Knowles would stop into the office this afternoon and maybe notice it. Maybe this would be the day when he'd suggest they might have dinner together. She had daydreamed like that only hours ago. How could everything change so quickly, so terribly . . . ?

"Mrs. Prentiss?"

"Yes. Oh, I'm sorry. I guess I'm a bit distracted today." To her ears she sounded falsely cheery. "As you can see, this kitchen needs modernizing, but it is very well laid out and roomy. That fireplace is large enough to cook for a crowd—but I'm sure you'd settle for modern ovens."

Unconsciously she'd lifted her voice. The wind was howling around the house with a harsh, mournful sound. From somewhere upstairs she heard a door slam and, just for a second, a wailing sound. It was her nerves; this house upset her today. The kitchen was freezing, too.

Quickly she led the way into the front rooms. She was anxious that Mr. Kragopoulos have the important first impression of the water view.

The savagery of the day only enhanced the breathtaking panorama that met their eyes when they stood at the windows. Angry whitecaps churned, lifted, fell, crashed on the rocks, pulled back. Together they stared at the tumultuous beating of the water on the rocks at the base of the cliff below.

"At high tide these rocks are completely covered," she said. "But just down a little to the left, past the jetty, there's a beautiful big sandy beach that is part of the property, and the dock is just past that."

She took him from room to room, pointing out the magnificent wide oak floors, the massive fireplaces, the leaded pane windows, the way the overall layout lent itself to a fine restaurant. They went up to the second floor, and he examined the large rooms that could be rented to overnight guests.

"During the renovation, they changed the small bedrooms into baths and connected them with the large rooms," Dorothy explained. "As a result, you've got really beautiful units that only need painting and papering. The brass beds alone are worth a fortune. Really, most of the furniture is very good—look at that highboy, for example. I used to have an interior decorator's shop, and a house like this is my idea of a dream to work on. The possibilities are endless."

He was interested. She could tell by the way he took time to open closet doors, pound walls and turn on water taps.

"The third floor has more bedrooms, and then Mr. Parrish's apartment is on the fourth floor," she said. "That apartment was designed for the resident manager of the country club. It's quite spacious and has a wonderful view of the town as well as the water."

He was pacing off the room and did not answer. Feeling pushy and garrulous, Dorothy walked over to the window. She should give him a chance to consider the house quietly and come up with any questions that might occur to him. *Hurry, hurry*, she thought. She wanted to get out of here. The insistent need to be back with Ray and Nancy, to know what was happening, was overwhelming. Suppose the children were out somewhere, exposed to this weather? Maybe she should take the car and cruise up and down; maybe they had just wandered away. Maybe if she tried to look in the woods, if she called them . . . She shook her head. She was being so foolish.

When Nancy had left Missy at the office with her yesterday, she'd said, "Please make her keep her mittens on when you go out. Her hands get so cold." Nancy had laughed as she handed Dorothy the mittens, saying, "As you can see, they don't match—and I'm not trying to set a style. This kid is always losing mittens." She'd given her one red mitten with a smile face and a blue-and-green-checked one.

Dorothy remembered the cheerful smile with which Missy had held up her hands when they'd gone for their drive. "Mommy said don't forget my mittens, Aunt Dorothy," she'd warned reproachfully. Later on, when they'd picked up Mike and stopped for ice cream, she'd asked, "Is it all right if I take my mittens off when I eat my cone?" Blessed little baby. Dorothy dabbed at the tears that rushed to her eyes.

Determinedly she composed herself and turned back to John Kragopoulos, who had just finished making notes on the size of the room. "You don't get high ceilings like these anymore except in these wonderful old houses," he exulted.

She couldn't tolerate being here like this any longer. "Let's go upstairs now," she said abruptly. "I think you'll like the view from the apartment." She led the way back into the hall and to the front staircase. "Oh, did you notice that there are four heat zones in this house? It saves a lot on fuel bills."

They walked up the two flights of stairs quickly. "The third floor is exactly like the second floor," she explained as they passed it. "Mr. Parrish has been renting the apartment on and off for six or seven years, I guess. His rent is quite minimal; but Mr. Eldredge felt that the presence of a tenant discourages vandals. Here we are—just down the hall." She knocked at the door of the apartment. There was no answer. "Mr. Parrish," she called. "Mr. Parrish."

She began to open her handbag. "That's strange. I can't imagine where he'd go without his car. But I've got a key here somewhere." She started to rummage through her bag, feeling unreasonable annoyance. Over the phone Mr. Parrish had obviously been unhappy that she was bringing someone over. If he had been going out, he might have told her. She hoped the apartment was tidy. There weren't that many people looking for a three-hundred-fifty-thousand-dollar investment. They hadn't had even a nibble on the property in nearly a year.

Dorothy did not realize that the handle was being turned from the inside. But when the door was pulled open abruptly, she looked up and gasped and stared into the searching eyes and perspiring face of the fourth-floor tenant, Courtney Parrish.

"What a dreadful day for you to have to come." Parrish's tone was courteous as he stepped aside to let them pass. By holding the door back and getting out of the way, he reasoned, he might be able to avoid shaking hands. He could feel that his hands were drenched in perspiration.

His eyes darted from one to the other. Had they heard the little girl—that one cry? He was such a fool . . . getting too eager. After the phone call, he'd had to hurry so much. Picking up the children's clothing, in his excitement he'd almost missed the little girl's undershirt. Then the can of baby powder had spilled. He'd had to wipe that up.

He'd taped the children's hands and feet and mouths and hidden them in that secret room behind the fireplace downstairs that he'd discovered months ago in wandering through the house. He knew those hidden rooms were peculiar to many old Cape houses. The early settlers used to hide in them during Indian attacks. But then he'd panicked. Suppose that fool of a real estate woman knew about that room and decided to show it? It was reached by a spring in the built-in bookcase in the main room downstairs.

Suppose she knew about it; just suppose. Even as Dorothy's Buick sedan pulled up and into the garage, he had dashed from his watching point at the window and rushed down to get the children. He'd carried them up and thrown them into one of the deep closets in the bedroom. Better . . . much better. He could say that he used that closet for storage and couldn't find the key. Since he had put a new lock on, that fool of a real estate woman couldn't possibly have a duplicate. Besides, the other closet in the room was practically the same size. She could show that one. That was where he could make a mistake . . . by getting complicated.

They'd dallied downstairs long enough for him to make one last inspection of the apartment; he hadn't missed anything, he was sure. The tub was still full, but he'd decided to leave it. He knew he'd sounded too annoyed over the phone. Let Dorothy think that that was the reason; he'd been just about to bathe. That would justify annoyance.

He wanted so much to get back to the little girl that it was painful. From deep in his loins he felt frantic desire. Right now, there she was, just a few feet from them all, behind that door, her little body half-naked. Oh, he couldn't wait! Be careful. Be careful. He tried to pay attention to the voice of reason that kept cautioning him, but it was so hard. . . .

"John Kragopoulos." That damn fellow was insisting on shaking his hand. Clumsily he tried to dry his palm on his trouser leg before grasping the outstretched hand that he could not ignore. "Courtney Parrish," he said sullenly.

He could see the fleeting expression of distaste come over the other man's face when their hands touched. Probably a damned fag. Half the restaurants on this side of the Cape were run by fags. Now they wanted this house too. Well, fine. After today he wouldn't need it.

Suddenly he realized that if this house were sold, no one would ever find it suspicious if as Courtney Parrish he didn't come back to the Cape. Then he could lose weight and let his hair grow and totally change his appearance again, because he would want to be here for Nancy's trial, after they found the children's bodies and accused her. Why, this wasn't a problem at all. Fate was playing into his hands. This was meant to be.

He shuddered as a wave of exhilaration surged through his body. Why, he could even ask about Nancy. It would be only neighborly.

Feeling suddenly confident, he said courteously, "I am pleased to meet you, Mr. Kragopoulos, and rue the weather in which you first observe this wonderful house." Miraculously, the dampness was leaving his hands and armpits and groin.

The tension in the small foyer relaxed tangibly. He realized that most of it was emanating from Dorothy anyway. Why not? He'd seen her countless times in these past years, in and out of the Eldredge house, pushing the children on the swing, taking them in her car. He had her number: one of those dreary middle-aged widows trying to be important to someone; a parasite. Husband dead. No children. A miracle she didn't have a sick old mother. Most of them did. That helped them to be martyrs to their friends. So nice to Mother. Why? Because they needed to be nice to someone. They had to be important. And if they had children, they concentrated on them. The way Nancy's mother had.

"I have been listening to the radio," he said to Dorothy, "and am so disturbed. Have the Eldredge children been found yet?"

"No." Dorothy felt all her nerve endings tingling. From inside she could hear that the radio was on. She caught the word "bulletin." "Excuse me," she cried, and hurried into the living room and over to the radio. Swiftly she turned up the volume. ". . . storm increasing. Gale winds from fifty to sixty miles an hour are predicted. Driving is hazardous. The air and water search for the Eldredge children has been suspended indefinitely. Special patrol cars will continue cruising in Adams Port and vicinity. Chief Coffin of Adams Port urges that anyone who believes he or she may have any information report it at once. He urges that any untoward incident be discussed with the police, such as a strange vehicle that may have been seen in the neighborhood of the Eldredge home; any unfamiliar person or persons in the area. Call this special number: KL five, three eight hundred. Your privacy will be respected."

The commentator's voice continued. "Despite the urgent appeal for clues to the missing children, we have it on good authority that Mrs. Nancy Harmon Eldredge will be taken to Police Head-quarters for questioning."

She had to go to Nancy and Ray. Dorothy turned to John Krago-poulos abruptly. "As you can see, this is a charming apartment quite suitable for two people. The view from both the front and back windows in this room is really spectacular."

"You are an astronomer, perhaps?" John Kragopoulos spoke to Courtney Parrish.

"Not really. Why do you ask?"

"It is just that magnificent telescope."

Belatedly, Parrish realized that the telescope was still positioned facing the Eldredge house. Seeing that John Kragopoulos was about to look through it he gave it an abrupt push so that it tilted upward.

"I enjoy studying the stars," he volunteered hastily.

John Kragopoulos squinted as he looked through the lens. "Mag-nificent equipment," he cried. "Simply magnificent." Carefully he manipulated the telescope until it was pointing in the same direction as it had been when he had first noticed it. Then, sensing the other man's antagonism, he straightened up and began to study the room. "This is a well-laid-out apartment," he commented to Dorothy.

"I have been most comfortable here," Parrish volunteered. In-wardly he was fuming at himself. Once more he had suspiciously overreacted. The moisture was pouring from his body again. Had he forgotten anything else? Was there any sign of the children around? Frantically his eyes darted around the room. Nothing.

Dorothy said, "I'd like to show the bedroom and bath if it's all right."

"Of course."

He'd straightened the coverlet on the bed and shoved the can of baby powder into the night-table drawer.

"The bathroom is as large as most of today's second bedrooms,"

Dorothy told John Kragopoulos. Then, as she glanced around it, she said, "Oh, I'm so sorry." She stared down at the filled tub. "We did catch you at an inconvenient time. You were just about to bathe."

"I have no rigid schedule to follow." Despite the words, he managed to leave the impression that she had indeed inconvenienced him.

John Kragopoulos stepped back into the bedroom hastily. He realized that this man obviously resented their coming. Leaving the tub like that was a clumsy way of making the point. And that duck floating in the tub. A child's toy. He winced, disgusted. His hand touched the closet door. The satiny quality of the wood intrigued him. Really, this house was beautifully constructed. John Kragopoulos was a hardheaded businessman, but he also believed in instinct. His instinct told him that this house would be a good investment. They wanted three hundred and fifty thousand for it. . . . He'd offer two ninety-five and come up to three twenty. He was sure he could get it for that.

The decision finalized in his mind, he began to take a proprietary interest in the apartment. "May I open this closet?" he asked. The question was perfunctory. He was already turning the handle.

"I'm sorry. I changed the lock on that closet and can't seem to find the key. If you'll look in this other closet . . . they're practically identical."

Dorothy looked sharply at the new handle and lock. Both were run-of-the-mill low-priced hardware-store items. "I do hope you kept the original handle," she said. "All the doorknobs were specially cast solid brass."

"Yes, I have it. It needs fixing." God, would that woman insist on turning the handle? Suppose the new lock gave? It wasn't a very tight fit into the old wood. Suppose it slid open?

Dorothy relaxed her grip on the handle. The slight flare of annoyance she'd felt vanished as quickly as it had come. What, in the name of heaven, difference did it make if all the brass handles all over the universe were changed? Who cared?

Parrish had to clamp his lips together to keep from ordering that nosy woman and her prospective buyer out. The children were just on the other side of the door. Had he tightened their gags enough? Would they hear the familiar voice and try to make some kind of sound? He had to get rid of these people.

But Dorothy wanted to go too. She was aware of an indefinably familiar scent in the bedroom—one that made her acutely aware of Missy. She turned to John Kragopoulos. "Perhaps we should start . . . if you're ready."

He nodded. "I'm quite ready, thank you." He started to leave, this time obviously avoiding shaking hands. Dorothy followed him. "Thank you, Mr. Parrish," she said hastily over her shoulder. "I'll be in touch with you."

She led the way down the stairs to the main floor in silence. They went through the kitchen, and when she opened the back door she could see why the gale warnings were in effect. The wind had heightened sharply in the brief time they'd been in the house. Oh, God, the children would die of exposure if they were outside all this time.

"We'd better make a dash for the garage," she said. John Kragopoulos, looking preoccupied, nodded and took her arm. Together they ran, not bothering to stay under the overhang. With the increased wind velocity there was simply no protection from the sleet, which was now finely blended with snow.

In the garage, Dorothy walked between the station wagon and her car and opened the door on the driver's side. As she began to slide into her car, she glanced down. A bright red scrap of material on the garage floor caught her eye. Getting out of the car again, she bent down, picked it up, then slumped back into the car seat holding the object against her cheek. John Kragopoulos, sounding alarmed, asked, "My dear Mrs. Prentiss, what is wrong?"

"It's the mitten!" Dorothy cried. "It's Missy's. She was wearing it yesterday when I took her out for ice cream. She must have left it in the car. I guess I kicked it out when I got out of the car before. She was always losing her mittens. She never had two on that matched. We always joked about that. And this morning, they found the mate of this one on the swing." Dorothy began to sob—a dry, hacking sound that she tried to stifle by holding the mitten against her lips.

John Kragopoulos said quietly, "There is little that I can say except to remind you that a merciful and loving God is aware of your pain and the agony of the parents. He will not fail your need. Somehow I am confident of that. Now, please, wouldn't you like me to drive?"

"Please," Dorothy said in a muffled voice. She pushed the mitten deep into her pocket as she slid over. She wouldn't want Nancy or Ray to see it; it would be too heartbreaking. Oh, Missy, Missy! She'd taken it off when she started to eat the cone yesterday. She could see her dropping it on the seat. Oh, the poor little kids.

John Kragopoulos was glad to be driving. A great restlessness had come over him in the room with that hideous man. There was something too slimy and sour-smelling about him. And that scent of baby powder in the bedroom and that incredible toy in the tub. How could a grown man need such trappings?

Upstairs, Parrish stood to one side and watched from the window until the car had disappeared around the bend in the lane. Then, with trembling fingers, he drew out the key from his pocket and unlocked the closet door.

The boy was conscious. His sandy hair fell on his forehead, and his large blue eyes were filled with terror as he stared mutely up. His mouth was still securely taped and his hands and legs still firmly tied.

Roughly he pushed the child aside and reached past him for the little girl. He lifted out her limp body and laid her on the bed—then shrieked in outrage and despair as he stared down at her closed eyes and pinched blue face. . . .

16

Nancy's hands were clenching and unclenching, pulling at the coverlet. Gently, Lendon covered her fingers with his own strong, well-shaped hands. Anxiety and agitation were causing her to breathe in harsh, labored breaths.

"Nancy, don't worry. Everyone here knows that you couldn't hurt your children. That's what you meant, isn't it?"

"Yes . . . yes . . . people think I could hurt them. How could I kill them? They are me. I died with them. . . ."

"We all die a little death when we lose the people we love, Nancy. Think back with me before all the trouble started. Tell me what it was like when you were growing up in Ohio."

"Growing up?" Nancy's voice trailed off into a whisper. The rigidity of her body began to relax.

"Yes, tell me about your father. I never knew him."

Jed Coffin moved restlessly, and the chair he was sitting on made a creaking sound against the wooden floor. Lendon shot him a warning glance. "I have reason for this," he said quietly. "Please bear with me."

"Daddy?" A lilt came into Nancy's voice. She laughed softly. "He was such fun. Mother and I used to drive to the airport to pick him up when he came in from a flight. In all those years he never came back from a trip without something for Mother and me. We used to go all over the world on his vacations. They always took me with them. I remember one trip . . ."

Ray could not take his eyes off Nancy. He had never heard her speak in that tone of voice—animated, amused, a ripple of laughter running through her words. Was this what he had been blindly trying to find in her? Was it more than being tired of living with the fear of discovery? He hoped so.

Jonathan Knowles listened intently to Nancy, approving of the technique Lendon Miles was using to gain her confidence and relax her before asking about the details of the day the Harmon children had vanished. It was agonizing to hear the soft ticking of the grandfather clock . . . a reminder that time was passing. He realized that he was finding it impossible not to look at Dorothy. He knew he had been harsh when he spoke to her as she was getting into her car. It was his disappointment that had reacted to her deliberate falsehood—the fact that she had made a point of telling him personally about knowing Nancy as a child.

Why had she done that? Was it perhaps that he had indicated somehow that Nancy looked familiar? Had it been simply an attempt to keep him from the truth because she couldn't trust him with the truth? Had he perhaps been displaying what Emily used to call his "Your witness, Counsel" manner?

In any event, he felt that he owed Dorothy an apology. She didn't look well. The strain was telling on her. She still was wearing her heavy coat, and her hands were jammed in her pockets. He decided that he wanted to talk to her at the first opportunity. She needed calming down. She certainly thought the world of those children.

The lights in the room flickered, then went off. "That figures." Jed Coffin propped the microphone on the table and searched for matches. Quickly Ray lighted the antique gas lamps on either side of the mantel. They threw a yellow glow that melted and blended with the vivid red flames of the fireplace, bathing the couch where Nancy was lying in a rosy glow and throwing deep shadows on the corners of the dark room.

It seemed to Ray that the steady tattooing of the sleet against the house and the moaning of the wind through the pines had intensified. Suppose the children were out somewhere in this weather . . . ? Last night he'd awakened hearing Missy cough. But when he went into her room, she'd been settled again in deep sleep, her cheek cupped in her palm. As he bent over to pull up her covers, she'd murmured, "Daddy" and stirred, but at the touch of his hand on her back she'd settled down again.

And Michael. He and Mike had gone for milk to Wiggins' Market—was it just yesterday morning? They'd arrived just as that tenant at The Lookout, Mr. Parrish, was leaving. The man had nodded pleasantly, but when he got into that old Ford wagon of his, Michael's face had wrinkled with distaste. "I don't like him," he'd said.

Ray almost smiled at the memory. Mike was a rugged little guy, but he had something of Nancy's distaste for ugliness, and no matter how you sliced it, Courtney Parrish was a clumsy, slow-moving, unattractive man.

Even the Wigginses had commented on him. After he left, Jack Wiggins said drily, "That fellow's about the slowest-moving human being I ever bumped into. He meanders around shopping like he's got all the time in the world."

Michael had looked reflective. "I never have enough time," he said. "I'm helping my dad refinish a desk for my room, and every time I want to keep working on it, I have to get ready for school."

"You've got quite an assistant there, Ray," Jack Wiggins had remarked. "I'll give him a job anytime; he sounds like a worker."

Mike had picked up the package. "I'm strong, too," he'd said. "I can carry things. I can carry my sister for a long time."

Ray ground his hands into fists. This was unreal, impossible. The children missing. Nancy sedated. What was she saying?

Her voice still had that eager lilt. "Daddy used to call Mother and me his girls. . . ." Her voice faltered.

"What is it, Nancy?" Dr. Miles asked. "Your father called you his little girl? Did that upset you?"

"No . . . no . . . no . . . he called us his girls. It was different . . . it was different . . . not like that at all. . . ." Her voice rose sharply in protest.

Lendon's voice was soothing. "All right, Nancy. Don't worry about that. Let's talk about college. Did you want to go away to school?"

"Yes . . . I really did . . . except . . . I was worried about Mother. . . ."

"Why did you worry about her?"

"I was afraid she'd be lonely—because of Daddy . . . and we'd sold the house; she was moving into an apartment. So much had changed for her. And she'd started a new job. But she liked working. . . . She said she wanted me to go. . . . She liked to say that today . . . today . . ."

"Today is the first day of the rest of your life," Lendon finished quietly. Yes, Priscilla had said that to him too. The day she came into the office after she'd put Nancy on the plane for school. She told him about still waving goodbye after the plane had taxied away toward the runway. Then her eyes had filled, and she'd smiled apologetically. "Look how ridiculous I am," she'd said, trying to laugh; "the proverbial mother hen."

"I think you're doing fine," Lendon had told her.

"It's just that when you think how your life can change . . . so incredibly. All of a sudden, a whole part, the most important part . . . is ended. But on the other hand, I think when you've had something quite wonderful . . . so very much happiness . . . you can't look back and regret. That's what I told Nancy today. . . .

I don't want her worrying about me. I want her to have a wonderful time in school. I said that we should both remember that motto: 'Today is the first day of the rest of our lives.'"

Lendon remembered that a patient had come into the office. At the time, he'd considered it a blessing; he'd been dangerously close to putting his arms around Priscilla.

". . . but it was all right," Nancy was saying, her voice still hesitant and groping. "Mother's letters were cheerful. She loved her job. She wrote a lot about Dr. Miles. . . . I was glad. . . ."

"Did you enjoy school, Nancy?" Lendon asked. "Did you have many friends?"

"At first, I liked the girls, and I dated a lot."

"How about your schoolwork? Did you like your subjects?"

"Oh, yes. They all came pretty easily . . . except bio. . . ."

Her tone changed—subtly became troubled. "That was harder. I never liked science but the college required it . . . so I took it. . . ."

"And you met Carl Harmon."

"Yes. He . . . wanted to help me with bio. He had me come to his office and he'd go over the work with me. He said I was dating too much and that I must stop or I'd be sick. He was so concerned . . . he even started giving me vitamins. He must have been right . . . because I was so tired . . . so much . . . and started to feel so depressed. . . . I missed Mother. . . ."

"But you knew you would be home over Christmas."

"Yes . . . and it didn't make sense. . . . All of a sudden . . . it got so bad . . . I didn't want to upset her . . . so I didn't write about it . . . but I think she knew. . . . She came out for a weekend . . . because she was worried about me . . . . I know it. . . . And then she was killed . . . because she came out to see me. . . . It was my fault . . . my fault. . . ." Her voice rose in a shriek of pain, then broke into a sob.

Ray started out of his chair, but Jonathan pulled him back.

The oil lamp flickered on Nancy's face. It was contorted with pain. "Mother!" she cried, "Oh, Mother . . . please don't be dead . . . live! Oh, Mother, please, please live. . . . I need you. . . . Mother, don't be dead . . . Mother . . ."

Dorothy turned her head, trying to bite back tears. No wonder Nancy had resented her remarks about being a surrogate grandmother to Missy and Michael. Why was she here? No one was even conscious or caring of her presence. She'd be more useful if she went out and made coffee. Nancy might want some later too. She should take off her coat. She couldn't. She felt too cold; so alone. She stared down for a moment at the hooked rug and watched as the pattern blurred before her eyes. Lifting her head, she met the inscrutable gaze of Jonathan Knowles and knew that he'd been watching her for some time.

". . . Carl helped you when your mother died. He was good to you?" Why was Lendon Miles dragging out this agony? What point was there in making Nancy relive this too? Dorothy started to her feet.

Nancy's answer was quiet. "Oh, yes. He was so good to me. . . . He took care of everything."

"And you married him."

"Yes. He said he'd take care of me. And I was so tired. He was so good to me. . . ."

"Nancy, you mustn't blame yourself for your mother's accident. That wasn't your fault."

"Accident?" Nancy's voice was speculative. "Accident? But it wasn't an accident. It wasn't an accident. . . ."

"Of course it was." Lendon's voice stayed calm, but he could feel the tightness of his throat muscles.

"I don't know . . . I don't know. . . ."

"All right; we'll talk about it later. Tell us about Carl."

"He was good to me. . . ."

"You keep saying that, Nancy. How was he good to you?"

"He took care of me. I was sick; he had to do so much for me. . . ."

"What did he do for you, Nancy?"

"I don't want to talk about that."

"Why, Nancy?"

"I don't. I don't. . . ."

"All right. Tell us about the children. About Peter and Lisa."

"They were so good. . . ."

"They were well behaved, you mean."

"They were so good . . . too good . . ."

"Nancy you keep saying 'good.' Carl was so good to you. And the children were good. You must have been very happy."

"Happy? I was so tired . . ."

"Why were you so tired?"

"Carl said I was so sick. He was so good to me."

"Nancy, you must tell us. How was Carl good to you?"

"He made sure I was getting better. He wanted me to get better. He said I had to be a good little girl."

"How did you feel sick, Nancy? What hurt you?"

"So tired . . . always so tired. . . . Carl helped me. . . ."

"Helped you how?"

"I don't want to talk about that."

"But you must, Nancy. What did Carl do?"

"I'm tired . . . I'm tired now. . . ."

"All right, Nancy. I want you to rest for a few minutes; then we'll talk some more. Just rest . . . just rest. . . ."

Lendon got up. Chief Coffin immediately took his arm and jerked his head toward the kitchen. As soon as they were out of the room, Chief Coffin spoke abruptly. "This isn't leading us anywhere. This could take hours and you're not going to find anything out. The girl blames herself for her mother's accident because the mother had made the trip to see her. It's that simple. Now, if you think you can find out anything else about the Harmon murders, get to it. Or else I question her at Headquarters."

"You can't force . . . She's starting to talk. . . . There's a great deal that even her subconscious doesn't want to face."

The Chief snapped: "And I don't want to face myself if there's any chance those kids are still alive and I've wasted precious time here."

"All right, I'll get to questioning her about this morning. But first, please, let me ask her about the day the Harmon children disappeared. If there is any link between the two, she may reveal it."

Chief Coffin looked at his watch. "God, it's almost four already. Whatever visibility there was all day will be gone in half an hour. Where is a radio? I want to hear the newscast."

"There's one in the kitchen, Chief." Bernie Mills, the patrolman on guard in the house, was an earnest, dark-haired man in his early thirties. He'd been on the force twelve years, and this was by far the most sensational case he'd ever known. Nancy Harmon. Nancy Eldredge was Nancy Harmon! Ray Eldredge's wife. It showed. You never knew what was going on inside people. Bernie had played on the same ball team summers with Ray Eldredge when they were little kids. Then Ray had gone to one of those fancy prep schools and Dartmouth College. He had never expected Ray would settle on the Cape when he finished service. But he did. When he married the girl who'd rented this house, everybody said that she was some looker. A few people commented that she kind of reminded you of someone.

Bernie remembered his own reaction to that talk. Lots of people look like someone else. His own uncle, a deadbeat and drunk who made his aunt's life miserable, was a dead ringer for Barry Goldwater. He glanced quickly out the window. The television news guys were all still out there, with their trucks and all their gear. Looking for a story. He wondered what they'd think if they knew Nancy Eldredge was injected with truth serum right now. Now, there was a story. He was anxious to get home to tell Jean about it. He wondered how she was doing. The baby had been teething last night; kept both of them up.

For a single, terrible minute Bernie wondered how it would feel if the little guy was missing on a day like this . . . out there somewhere . . . and he not knowing. The prospect was so awful, so breathtaking, so mindshattering that he rejected it. Jean never took her eyes off Bobby. Sometimes she bugged Bernie the way she was always fussing about the kid. Right now her need to never take her eyes off their baby reassured him, assuaged his apprehensions. The little guy was fine—trust Jean.

Dorothy was in the kitchen filling the coffeepot. Bernie reflected that Dorothy bugged him a little. She had such a—well, guess you'd call it reserved—way. She could be nice and friendly—but, well, Bernie didn't know. He decided that Dorothy was just a little too highfalutin for his thinking.

He turned on the transistor radio, and instantly the voice of Dan Phillips, the newscaster for WCOD in Hyannis, filled the room. "The case of the missing Eldredge children has just taken a new twist," Phillips said, and his voice was pulsing with somewhat unprofessional excitement. "A mechanic, Otto Linden from the Gulf Station on Route Twenty-eight in Hyannis, has just phoned us to say that he can positively state that this morning at nine A.M. he filled the gas tank of Rob Legler, the missing witness in the Harmon murder case of seven years ago. Mr. Linden said that Legler appeared nervous and volunteered the information that he was on his way to Adams Port to visit someone who probably wouldn't be glad to see him. He was driving a late-model red Dodge Dart."

Jed Coffin swore softly. "And I'm wasting my time here listening to this claptrap." He started for the phone and picked it up just as it rang. After the caller identified himself, he said impatiently, "I heard it. All right. I want a roadblock on the bridges going to the mainland. Check with the FBI deserter file—find out what they may know about the latest whereabouts of Rob Legler. Put out a bulletin about a red Dodge." He slammed the receiver back onto the hook and turned to Lendon. "Now I've got a simple, direct question for you to ask Mrs. Eldredge. It's whether or not Rob Legler got here this morning . . . and what he said to her."

Lendon stared. "You mean . . ."

"I mean that Rob Legler is the person who could dump Nancy Eldredge back into the middle of a murder trial. The Harmon case has never been closed. Now, suppose he's been hiding out in Canada for six years or so. He needs money. Didn't it come out at the Harmon trial that Nancy had inherited a fair amount of money from her parents?—some hundred and fifty thousand dollars. Now, suppose Rob Legler knows about that money and somehow finds out where Nancy is. The District Attorney's staff in San Francisco know where she's been. Now, suppose Legler decides he's sick of Canada and wants to come back here and needs a stake. How about going to Nancy Eldredge and promising to change his testimony if he's ever caught and there's a new trial? That's the same as making her give him a blank check for the rest of her life. He gets here. He sees her. The deal sours. She doesn't go for it . . . or he changes his mind. She knows that at any moment he may be caught or turn himself in and she's back in San Francisco on a murder charge, and she cracks. . . ."

"And murders her Eldredge children?" Lendon's voice was scornful. "Have you thought about the possibility that this student who nearly put Nancy in the gas chamber was in the vicinity when both sets of children disappeared?

"Give me one more chance," Lendon pleaded. "Just let me ask

her about the day the Harmon children disappeared. I want her to describe the events of that day first."

"You have thirty minutes—no more."

Dorothy began pouring coffee into cups that she'd already placed on a tray. Quickly she cut up a coffee cake that Nancy had baked the day before. "Perhaps coffee will help everyone," she said.

She carried the tray into the front room. Ray was sitting in the chair Lendon had drawn next to the couch. He was holding Nancy's hands in his, gently massaging them. She was very still. Her breathing was even, but as the others came into the room, she stirred and moaned.

Jonathan was standing by the mantel, staring into the fire. He had lighted his pipe, and the warm smell of the good tobacco he used had begun to penetrate the room. Dorothy breathed it in deeply as she set the coffee tray on the round pine table by the fireplace. A wave of pure nostalgia washed over her. Kenneth had smoked a pipe, and that had been his brand of tobacco. She and Kenneth used to love stormy winter afternoons like this. They would make a roaring fire and get out wine and cheese and books and sit contently together. Regret swept over her. Regret because you really can't control your life. Most of the time you don't act; you react.

"Will you have coffee and cake?" she asked Jonathan.

He looked at her thoughtfully. "Please."

She knew he took cream and one sugar. Without asking, she prepared the coffee that way and handed it to him. "Shouldn't you take your coat off?" he asked her.

"In a little while. I'm still so chilled."

Dr. Miles and Chief Coffin had followed her in and were helping themselves to the coffee. Dorothy poured another cup and carried it over to the couch. "Ray, please have some."

He looked up. "Thank you." As he reached for it, he murmured to Nancy, "Everything is going to be all right, little girl."

Nancy shuddered violently. Her eyes flew open and she threw up her arm, knocking the cup from Ray's hand. It fell and broke on the floor, spewing hot liquid over her robe and the blanket. Splashes of it spattered on Ray and Nancy. Simultaneously they winced as Nancy cried out in the desperate tone of a trapped animal, "I am not your little girl! Don't call me your little girl!"

17

Courtney Parrish turned from the small unmoving figure on the bed, sighing heavily. He'd taken the adhesive from Missy's mouth and the cords from her wrists and ankles, and they made an untidy pile on the quilt. Her fine, silky hair was matted now. He'd been planning to brush it when he bathed her, but now there was no point. He needed her response.

The little boy, Michael, was still on the floor of the closet. His large blue eyes were terrified as Courtney picked him up and hugged him against his massive chest.

He laid Michael on the bed, undid the bindings on his ankles and wrists and with a quick pull yanked the adhesive off his mouth. The boy cried out in pain, then bit his lip. He seemed more responsive—infinitely wary, apprehensive, but with some of the courage of the trapped animal.

"What did you do to my sister?" The belligerent tone made Courtney realize that the boy hadn't drunk all the milk with the sedative he'd given him just before the meddling fools came along.

"She's asleep."

"Let us go home. We want to go home. I don't like you. I told my daddy I didn't like you, and Aunt Dorothy was here and you hid us."

Courtney lifted his right hand, curved it into the mitt-like shape and slapped Michael across the cheek. Michael jerked back in pain and then rolled out from under the man's grasp. Courtney reached for him, lost his balance and fell clumsily across the bed. His mouth touched Missy's tangled yellow hair, and for an instant he was distracted. Pulling himself up, he turned and was on his feet, crouching to spring at Michael. But Michael was backing away toward the bedroom door. With a swift movement he opened it and raced through the adjoining sitting room.

Courtney lunged after him, realizing that he hadn't locked the apartment door. He hadn't wanted Dorothy to hear the distinct ping of the lock turning as she went downstairs.

Michael threw open the door and raced for the staircase. His shoes clattered on the uncarpeted stairs. He moved swiftly, a slim shadow that darted down into the protecting gloom of the third floor. Courtney hurried after him, but in his frantic rush lost his balance and fell. He hurtled down six steps before he managed to stop the fall by grasping the heavy wooden banister. Shaking his head to clear it, he picked himself up, aware of a sharp pain in his right ankle. He had to make sure the kitchen door was locked.

There was no further sound of footsteps. The boy was probably hiding in one of the third-floor bedrooms, but he had plenty of time to look for him. First the kitchen door. The windows were no problem. They were all double-locked, and too heavy anyhow. The double lock on the front door was too high for the child. He'd just secure the kitchen door, then search for the boy—room by room. He'd call to him and warn him. The boy was so frightened. His eyes had been so terrified and wary. He looked more than ever like Nancy this way. Oh, this was so unexpectedly wonderful. But he had to hurry. He had to make sure the boy couldn't get out of the house.

"I'll be right back, Michael," he called. "I'll find you. I'll find you, Michael. You're a very bad boy. You must be punished, Michael. Do you hear me, Michael?"

He thought he heard a noise in the bedroom on his right and rushed in, favoring his ankle. But the room was empty. Suppose the boy had run through this hallway and used the front stairs? Suddenly panicking, he lumbered down the remaining two flights. From outside he could hear the waves from the bay crashing against the rocks. He raced into the kitchen and over to the door. This was the door he always used going into and out of the house. This one had not only a double lock but a high bolt. His breath came in quick furious gasps. With thick, trembling fingers, he shoved the bolt into place. Then he pulled over a heavy wooden kitchen chair and wedged it under the knob. The boy would never be able to move this. There was no other way out of the house.

The heavy storm had almost obliterated the remaining daylight. Courtney switched on the overhead light, but an instant later it flickered and went off. He realized that the storm had probably pulled down some wires. It would make it harder to find the boy. All the upstairs bedrooms were fully furnished. They all had closets, too—deep ones—and cupboards that he might hide in. Courtney bit his lip in fury as he reached for the hurricane lamp on the table, struck the match and lighted the wick. The glass was red, and the light cast an eerie reddish glow against the fireplace wall and faded planked floor and thick-beamed ceiling. The wind wailed against the shutters as Courtney called, "Michael . . . it's all right, Michael. I'm not angry anymore. Come out, Michael. I'll take you home to your mother."

18

The chance to blackmail Nancy Harmon was the break Rob Legler had been needing for over six years—from the day he'd gotten on a plane to Canada after carefully shredding his embarkation orders for Vietnam. During those years, he'd worked as a farmhand near Halifax. It was the only job he'd been able to get, and he loathed it. Not for a minute did he regret his decision to bolt the Army. Who in the hell wanted to go to a filthy, hot hole to be shot at by a bunch of pint-sized bastards? He didn't.

He'd worked on the farm in Canada because he didn't have any alternative. He'd left San Francisco with sixty bucks in his pocket. If he went back home, he'd be tossed in jail. A conviction for desertion wasn't his idea of the way to spend the rest of his life. He needed a good stake to cut out for someplace like Argentina. He wasn't just one of the thousands of deserters who eventually might be able to slip back into the States with faked identification. Thanks to that blasted Harmon case, he was a hunted man.

If only that conviction hadn't been upset . . . that case would be finished. But that bastard of a D.A. had said if he spent twenty years he'd retry Nancy Harmon for the murder of those kids. And Rob was the witness, the witness who supplied the motive.

Rob couldn't let that scene happen again. As it was, the D.A. last time had told the jury that there was probably more to the

killing than Nancy Harmon wanting to get out of a home situation. "She was probably in love," he'd said. "We have here a very
attractive young woman who since the age of eighteen has been
married to an older man. Her life might well be the envy of many
a young woman. Professor Harmon's devotion to his young wife
and family was an example for the community. But is Nancy Harmon satisfied? No. When a student-repairman comes in, sent by
her husband so that she will not have to endure even a few hours'
discomfort, what does she do? She follows him around, insists he
have coffee, says it's nice to talk to someone young . . . says she has
to get away . . . responds passionately to his overtures . . . and then
when he tells her that 'raising kids isn't his bag' she calmly prom-
ises him that her children are going to be smothered.

"Now, ladies and gentlemen of the jury, I despise Rob Legler. I
believe that he toyed with this foolish young woman. I don't for a
minute believe that their unholy passion ended with a few kisses . . .
but I do believe him when he quotes the damning phrases that fell
from Nancy Harmon's lips."

Frig him. Rob felt sick fear in the pit of his stomach whenever
he remembered that speech. That bastard would have given anything to have made him an accessory to murder. All because he'd
been in old Harmon's office the day his wife phoned to tell him
the heater had gone off. Rob wasn't usually given to volunteering
his services. But he'd never seen a machine or engine or piece of
equipment he couldn't fix, and he'd heard some guys talk about
what a doll that creepy old drag had for a wife.

That piece of intriguing information had made him volunteer
his services. At first Harmon had turned him down, but then when
he couldn't get his regular maintenance man he'd said okay. He
said he didn't want his wife taking the kids to a motel. That was
what she'd suggested.

So Rob had gone over. Everything the guys had said about

Nancy Harmon was true. She was a real looker. But she sure didn't seem to know it. She was kind of hesitant . . . unsure of herself. He'd gotten over about noon. She was just feeding the two little kids . . . a boy and a girl. Quiet kids, both of them. She didn't pay much attention to him, just thanked him for coming and turned back to the kids.

He realized that the only way to get her attention was through the kids and started talking to them. It was always easy for Rob to turn on the charm. He liked gals older than himself, too. Not that this one was older by much. But he'd learned from the time he was sixteen and screwing his next-door neighbor's wife that if you're nice to a woman's kids, she thinks you're A-okay and all the guilt goes down the drain. Boy, Rob could write a book on the whole mother-complex rationalization.

In a couple of minutes he'd had the kids laughing and Nancy laughing, and then he'd invited the little boy down to be his helper fixing the furnace. Just as he expected, the little girl asked to go too, and then Nancy said she'd come along to make sure they didn't get in the way. There wasn't much wrong with the furnace—just a clogged filter—but he said it needed a part and he could get it working but he'd be back and do the job right.

He got out fast the first day. No point in getting old Harmon upset. Went straight back to his office. Harmon looked annoyed and worried when he opened the door, but when he saw Rob he gave a big, relieved smile. "So soon? You must be a whiz. Or couldn't you take care of it?"

Rob said, "I got it going. But you need a new part, sir, that I'll be glad to pick up. It's one of those little things that if you call in a regular service, they'll make a big production over. I can get the part for a couple of bucks. Be glad to do it."

Harmon fell for it, of course. Probably glad to save the money. And Rob went back the next day and the next day. Harmon warned him that his wife was very nervous and rested a lot and to please keep out of her way. But Rob didn't see where she acted nervous. Timid, maybe, and scared. He got her talking. She told him that she'd had a nervous breakdown after her mother died. "I guess I've been terribly depressed," she said. "But I'm sure I'm getting better. I've even stopped taking most of my medicine. My husband doesn't realize that. He'd probably be annoyed. But I feel better without it."

Rob had told her how pretty she was, kind of feeling his way. He'd begun to suspect that she might be a pushover. It was obvious she was pretty bored with old Harmon and getting restless. He said maybe she should get out more. She'd said, "My husband doesn't believe in company. He feels that at the end of the day he doesn't need to see any more people—not after all the students he has to contend with."

That was when he'd known he'd try to make a pass at her.

Rob had an airtight alibi for that morning the Harmon kids had disappeared. He'd been in a class of only six students. But the D.A. had told him that if he could find one shred of evidence that would help him hang an accessory charge on Rob, it would be his pleasure to do it. Rob had hired a lawyer. Plenty scared, he didn't want the D.A. poking into his background and finding out about the time he'd been named in a paternity suit in Cooperstown. The lawyer had told him that his posture had to be that he was the respectful student of a distinguished professor; had been anxious to do a favor for him; had tried to stay away from the wife, but she had kept following him around. That he never took it seriously when she talked about the children being smothered. Actually, he'd thought she was just nervous and sick, the way the Professor had warned him.

But on the stand it didn't work like that. "Were you attracted to this young woman?" the D.A. asked smoothly.

Rob looked at Nancy sitting at the defendant's table next to her lawyer, looking at him through blank, unseeing eyes. "I didn't think in those terms, sir," he replied. "To me Mrs. Harmon was the wife of a teacher I admired greatly. I simply wanted to fix the furnace as I'd volunteered to do and get back to my room. I had a paper to write, and anyhow a sick woman with two children simply isn't my bag." It was that elaboration, that last damned phrase that the D.A. had pounced on. By the time he was finished with him, Rob was wringing with perspiration.

Yes, he'd heard the Professor's wife was a doll. . . . No, he wasn't given to volunteering his help. . . . Yes, he'd been curious to get a look at her. . . . Yes, he had made a pass at her. . . .

"But it stopped there!" Rob had shouted from the stand. "With two thousand coeds on campus, I didn't need problems." Then he'd admitted that he had told Nancy that she turned him on and he'd like to hustle her.

The D.A. had looked at him contemptuously, then read into the record the time Rob had been beaten up by an irate husband — the episode in Cooperstown when he'd been named in the paternity suit.

The D.A. said, "This philanderer was no willing volunteer. He went into that house to size up a beautiful young woman whom he'd heard about. He made a play for her. It succeeded beyond his wildest dreams. Ladies and gentlemen of the jury, I am not suggesting that Rob Legler was part of the scheme to murder Nancy Harmon's children. At least, in the legal sense he wasn't. But I am convinced that morally, before God, he is guilty. He let this gullible, ungrateful young woman know that he'd—and I use his words—'hustle her' if she were free, and she chose a freedom that is repugnant to the basic instincts of mankind. She murdered her children to be free of them."

After Nancy Harmon was sentenced to die in the gas chamber,

Professor Harmon had committed suicide. He drove his car to the same beach where one of the kids had been found and left it by the shore. He pinned a note to the wheel saying that it was all his fault. He should have realized how sick his wife was. He should have taken his children from her. He was responsible for their deaths and her action. "I tried to play God," he wrote. "I loved her so dearly that I thought I could cure her. I thought bearing children would turn her mind from the grief of her mother's death. I thought love and care would heal her, but I was wrong; I meddled beyond my depth. Forgive me, Nancy."

There hadn't been any roar of approval when the conviction was overturned. It happened because two women jurors had been heard discussing the case in a bar midway through the trial and saying she was guilty as sin. But by the time a new trial was ordered Rob had graduated, been drafted, given Vietnam orders and bolted. Without him, the D.A. had no case and had to let Nancy go—but swore he'd retry her the day he could get hold of Rob again.

Over the years in Canada, Rob had thought of that trial often. There was something that bothered him about the whole setup. Taking himself out of it, he didn't buy Nancy Harmon as a murderess. She'd been like a clay pigeon in court. Harmon certainly hadn't helped her, breaking down on the stand when he was supposed to be in the midst of saying what a great mother she was.

In Canada, Rob was something of a celebrity among the draft evaders he hung out with whom he'd told about the case. They'd asked about Nancy, and Rob told them what a dish she was . . . hinting that he'd had a little action. He showed them the press clippings of the trial and Nancy's pictures.

He told them that she had to have some dough—that it came out at the trial that her folks left her over a hundred and fifty grand; that if he could find her he'd put the arm on her for money to split to Argentina.

Then he got his break. One of his buddies, Jim Ellis, who knew about his connection with the Harmon case, slipped home to visit his mother, who had terminal cancer. The mother lived in Boston, but because the FBI was watching the house hoping to pick up Jim, she met him in Cape Cod in a cottage she had hired on Maushop Lake. When Jim got back to Canada, he was bursting with news. He asked Rob what it would be worth to him to know where he could find Nancy Harmon.

Rob was skeptical until he saw the picture Jimmy had managed to snap of Nancy on the beach. There was no mistaking her. Jim had done some digging, too. The background checked. He'd found out that her husband was pretty prosperous. Quickly they worked out a deal. Rob would get to see Nancy. Tell her that if she'd stake him to fifty thousand bucks, he'd split to Argentina and she'd never have to worry about him testifying against her. Rob reasoned that she'd go for it, especially now that she was remarried and had more kids. It was a cheap price for her to know that someday she wouldn't be haul-assed back to California to stand trial.

Jim wanted a flat twenty percent for his share. While Rob was seeing Nancy, Jim would arrange for phony Canadian passports, identification and reservations to Argentina. They were available for a price.

They laid their plans carefully. Rob managed to rent a car from an American kid who was in school in Canada. He shaved his beard and cut his hair for the trip. Jim warned him that the minute you looked like a hippie, every damn cop in those crappy New England towns was ready to clock you with radar.

Rob decided to drive straight through from Halifax. The less time he spent in the States, the less chance of getting picked up. He timed his arrival at the Cape for early in the morning. Jim had found out that Nancy's husband always opened his office about nine-thirty. He'd get to her house around ten. Jim had made a map of her street for him, including that driveway through the woods. He could hide the car there.

He was running low on gas when he hit the Cape. That was why he got off at Hyannis to refuel. Jim had told him that even out of season there were a lot of tourists there. He'd be less likely to be noticed. All the way down he'd been nervous, trying to decide if he should offer his deal to Nancy and her husband together. Likely he'd have to know about her getting a bundle of cash. But suppose this guy called the cops? Rob would be convicted of desertion and blackmail. No, it was better to talk directly to Nancy. She must still remember sitting at that defendant's table.

The attendant at the gas station was helpful. Checked everything over, cleaned the windows, put air in the tires without being asked. That was why Rob was off guard. When he was settling the bill, the attendant asked if he was down for some fishing. That was when he babbled that he was actually doing some hunting—going to Adams Port to see an old girlfriend who might not be glad to see him. Then, cursing his talkiness, he bolted, stopping at a nearby diner for some breakfast.

He drove into Adams Port at quarter of ten. Slowly cruising around, studying the map Jim had drawn for him, he got a feel of the layout. Even so he almost missed the dirt road leading to the woods behind her property. He realized that after he slowed up for that old Ford wagon pulling out from it. Backing up, he turned into the dirt road, parked the car and started walking to the rear door of Nancy's house. That was when she'd come running out like a madwoman shrieking those names. Peter, Lisa, those were the dead kids. He followed her through the woods to the lake and watched when she threw herself into the water. He was just about to go after her when she dragged herself out and fell on the beach. He knew she looked in his direction. He wasn't sure if she saw him, but he did know that he had to get out of there. He didn't know what was happening, but he didn't want to get involved.

Back in the car, he'd cooled off. Maybe she'd turned into a drunk. If she was still screaming for the dead kids, chances were that she'd jump at the chance to know she didn't have to worry about a new trial. He decided to check into some motel in Adams Port and try to see her again the next day.

In the motel, Rob promptly went to bed and fell asleep. He awakened late in the afternoon and switched on the television set to catch the news. The screen focused in time for him to see a picture of himself and a voice describing him as the missing witness in the Harmon murder case. Numbly, Rob listened as the announcer recapped the disappearance of the Eldredge children. For the first time in his life he felt trapped. Now that he'd shaved off his beard and shortened his hair, he looked exactly the way he had in the picture.

If Nancy Eldredge had actually killed her new family, who would believe that he hadn't had something to do with it? It must have happened just before he got there. Rob thought of the old Ford wagon that had backed out from the dirt road just before he turned in. Massachusetts license, first two numbers 8-6 . . . heavy-set guy behind the wheel.

But he couldn't talk about that even if he got caught. Couldn't admit being at the Eldredge house this morning. Who would believe him if he told the truth? Rob Legler's instinct for self-preservation told him to get off Cape Cod, and it was a cinch he couldn't go in a bright red Dodge that every cop was looking for.

He packed his bag and slipped out the back door of the motel. A Volks Beetle was parked in the stall next to the Dodge. Through the window he'd noticed the couple who had left it: They'd checked in just before he turned on the news. Chances were, if he was any judge, they were good for a couple of hours. No one else was outside braving the sleet and wind.

Rob opened the engine lid of the Volks, connected a few wires and drove away. He'd use Route 6A heading for the bridge. With any luck, in half an hour he'd be off the Cape.

Six minutes later, he ran a red light. Thirty seconds after that, he glanced in the rearview mirror and saw a flashing red light reflected there. He was being chased by a police car. For an instant he considered surrendering himself; then the overwhelming need to bolt from trouble overcame him. As he rounded a corner, Rob slipped open the door, wedged the accelerator down with his suitcase and jumped out. He was disappearing into the wooded area behind stately Colonial homes when the police car, its siren now screaming, chased the wildly careening Volkswagen down the sloping road.

19

When Michael began to run down the stairs, he was sure that Mr. Parrish would catch him. But then he heard the terrible thumping that meant Mr. Parrish had fallen down the stairs. Michael knew that if he wanted to get away from Mr. Parrish he mustn't make any noise. He remembered the time Mommy had had the carpet on the stairs at home taken off. "Now, until the new treads go down, you kids have to play a new game," she'd said. "It's called civilized walking." Michael and Missy had made a game of walking down the side of the stairs near the banister on tiptoe. They got so good at it they used to sneak down and scare each other. Now, walking lightly that same way, Michael slipped noiselessly down to the first floor. He heard Mr. Parrish calling his name, saying he would find him.

He knew he had to get out of this house. He had to run down the winding road to the long road that led to Wiggins' Market. Michael hadn't decided whether he'd go into Wiggins' Market or run past it across Route 6A up the road that led to his house. He had to get Daddy and bring him back here for Missy.

Yesterday in Wiggins' Market he had told Daddy he didn't like Mr. Parrish. Now he was afraid of him. Michael felt the choking fear as he ran through the dark house. Mr. Parrish was a bad man. That was why he had tied them up and hidden them in the closet.

That was why Missy was so scared she couldn't wake up. Michael had tried to touch Missy in the closet. He knew she was scared. But he couldn't get his hands free. From inside the closet, he could hear Aunt Dorothy's voice. But she hadn't asked for them. She was right there and didn't guess that they were there. He was very angry that Aunt Dorothy didn't know they needed her. She should have guessed.

It was getting so dark. It was hard to see. At the bottom of the stairs, Michael looked around, confused, then darted toward the back of the house. He was in the kitchen. The outside door was over there. He rushed to it and reached for the knob. He was just about to turn the lock when he heard the footsteps approaching. Mr. Parrish. His knees trembled. If the door stuck, Mr. Parrish would grab him. Quickly, noiselessly, Michael raced out the other kitchen door, across the small foyer and into the little back parlor. He heard Mr. Parrish bolt the kitchen door. He heard him drag the chair over to it. The light in the kitchen was snapped on, and Michael shrank behind the heavy overstuffed couch. Crouching quietly, he barely fitted into the space between the couch and the wall. Dust from the couch tickled his nose. He wanted to sneeze. The light in the kitchen and hallway went out suddenly, and the house was black dark. He heard Mr. Parrish walking around, striking a match.

A moment later there was a reddish glow in the kitchen, and he heard Mr. Parrish call, "It's all right, Michael. I'm not angry anymore. Come out, Michael. I'll take you home to your mother."

20

John Kragopoulos had intended to drive directly to New York after leaving Dorothy, but a vague sense of depression coupled with a headache over the bridge of his nose made the five-hour trip seem suddenly insurmountable. It was the frightful weather, of course, and the intense distress Dorothy was suffering couldn't help transmitting itself. She had shown him the picture she carried in her wallet, and the thought of those beautiful children having met with foul play left a sickening feeling in the pit of his stomach.

But what an incredible thought, he mused. There was still the possibility the children had simply wandered away. How could anyone hurt a child? John thought of his own twenty-eight-year-old twin sons—one an Air Force pilot, the other an architect. Fine young men, both of them. A source of pride for a father. Long after he and their mother were gone, they would live. They were a part of his immortality. Suppose when they were babies, he had lost them. . . .

He was driving down Route 6A toward the mainland. Ahead on the right an attractive restaurant was set back from the road. The lighted sign, THE STAGEWAY, was a welcoming beacon in the afternoon gloom. Instinctively, John swung off the road and into the parking lot. He realized that it was nearly three o'clock and he had had exactly one cup of coffee and one piece of toast all day.

The bad weather had made the driving up from New York so slow he had been forced to skip lunch.

He rationalized that it was common sense to have a decent meal before he attempted the trip. And it was good business sense to try to strike up a conversation with the personnel of a large restaurant in a vicinity he was considering. He might be able to garner some useful information on the probable trade in the area.

Subconsciously approving of the rustic interior of the restaurant, he went directly to the bar. There were no customers at it, but that wasn't unusual before five o'clock in a town like this. He ordered a Chivas Regal on the rocks; then, when the bartender brought it, he asked if it would be possible to get something to eat.

"No problem." The bartender was about forty, dark-haired, with exaggerated muttonchops. John liked both his obliging answer and the way he kept the bar immaculately neat. A menu was produced. "If you feel like steak, the special sirloin is great," he volunteered. "Technically, the kitchen is closed between two-thirty and five, but if you don't mind eating right here . . ."

"Sounds perfect." Quickly John ordered the steak rare and a green salad. The Chivas warmed his body, and some of his depression began to lift. "You make a good drink," he said.

The bartender smiled. "It takes real talent to put together a Scotch on the rocks," he said.

"I'm in the business. You know what I mean." John decided to be candid. "I'm thinking of buying the place they call The Lookout for a restaurant. What's your top-of-the-head opinion?"

The other man nodded emphatically. "Could work. A real class restaurant, I mean. Here we do fine, but we get the middle-buck crowd. Families with kids. Old ladies on pensions. Tourists heading for the beach or antique shops. We're right on the main drag. But a place like The Lookout overlooking the bay . . . good atmosphere, good booze, a good menu . . . you could charge top dollar and keep it packed."

"That's my feeling."

"Of course, if I was you, I'd get rid of that old creep on the top floor."

"I was wondering about him. He seems to be somewhat odd."

"Well, he's supposed to be up here every year around this time for the fishing. I know because Ray Eldredge happened to mention it. Nice guy, Ray Eldredge. He's the one whose kids are missing."

"I heard about that."

"Damn shame. Nice little kids. Ray and Mrs. Eldredge bring them in here once in a while. Some looker, Ray's wife. But like I was saying, I'm not a native. I quit bartending in New York ten years ago after the third time I was mugged going home late. But I always been crazy for fishing. That's how I ended here. And one day just a few weeks ago, this big guy comes in and orders a drink. I know who he is, I seen him around. He's the tenant at The Lookout. Well, I try to make anybody relax, get his beefs off his chest, so just to make conversation, I ask him if he was here in September when the blues were running. You know what that stupe said?"

John waited.

"Nothing. Blank. Zero. He didn't have a clue." The bartender stood with his hands on his hips. "Do you believe anyone can come fishing to the Cape seven years and not know what I meant?"

The steak arrived. Gratefully John began to eat. It was delicious. As the taste of the prime meat combined with the warm glow of the drink, he relaxed perceptibly and began to think about The Lookout.

What the bartender had told him had confirmed his decision to make an offer on the place.

He had enjoyed going through the house. The sense of discomfort he'd experienced had begun only on the top floor. That was it. He had been uneasy in the apartment of the tenant, Mr. Parrish.

John finished the steak thoughtfully and rather abstractedly paid his bill, remembering to tip the bartender generously. Turning up his collar, he left the restaurant and headed for his car. Now he should turn right and keep toward the mainland? But for minutes he sat irresolutely in the car. What was the matter with him? He was acting like a fool. What crazy impulse was forcing him to return to The Lookout?

Courtney Parrish had been nervous. John had been too many years in the business of sizing people up not to know nervous tension when he saw it. That man had been worried . . . desperately anxious for them to leave. Why? There had been a heavy, sour sweaty smell on him . . . the smell of fear . . . but fear of what? And that telescope. Parrish had rushed over to change the direction it was pointing in when John bent over it. John remembered that when he put it back to approximately where it had been, he'd been able to see the police cars around the Eldredge home. Such an incredibly powerful telescope. If it was directed into the windows of homes in the town, anyone looking into it could become a peeping tom . . . a voyeur.

Was it possible that Courtney Parrish had been looking through the telescope when the children disappeared from behind their home . . . that he had seen something? But if he had, of course he would have called the police.

The car was cold. John turned the ignition key and waited for the engine to warm up before switching on the heater. He reached for a cigar and lighted it with the small gold Dunhill lighter that had been his wife's anniversary present to him: an extravagant, deeply cherished gift. He puffed at the cigar until the tip began to glow.

He was a fool. A suspicious fool. What did one do? Phone the police and say that a man seemed nervous and they should look into it? And if they did, Courtney Parrish would probably say, "I was about to take my bath and disliked having such short notice of the house being shown." Perfectly reasonable. People who lived alone tended to become precise in their habits.

Alone. That was the word. That was what was nagging John. He had been surprised not to see someone else in the apartment. Something had made him sure that Courtney Parrish was not alone.

It was the child's toy in the tub. That was it. That incredible rubber duck. And the cloying scent of baby powder . . .

A suspicion so absurd that it would be impossible to vocalize took shape in John Kragopoulos' mind.

He knew what he had to do. Deliberately he took his gold lighter from his pocket and hid it in the glove compartment of his car.

He would drive back to The Lookout unannounced. When Courtney Parrish answered the door, he would ask permission to look for his valuable lighter, which he must have dropped somewhere in the house during his inspection. It was a plausible request. It would give him a chance to look around carefully and either allay what was probably a ridiculous suspicion or have something more than suspicion to discuss with the police.

Having made up his mind, John stepped on the accelerator and swung the car left on Route 6A, back toward the center of Adams Port and the curving, hilly road that led to The Lookout. Visions of a faded, peeling rubber duck bobbed in his head as he drove through the steadily pelting sleet.

21

She didn't want to remember . . . there was only pain in going back. Once when she was very little, Nancy had reached up and pulled the handle of a pot on the stove. She could still remember how great torrents of bright red tomato soup had gushed over on her. She'd been in the hospital for weeks and still had faint scars on her chest.

. . . Carl had asked her about those scars . . . stroked them . . . "Poor little girl, poor little girl. . . ." He liked her to tell him about the incident over and over. "Did it hurt very much?" he would ask.

Remembering was like that. . . . Pain . . . only pain. . . . Don't remember . . . forget . . . forget. . . . Don't want to remember. . . .

But the questions, persistent, far away . . . asking about Carl . . . about Mother . . . Lisa . . . Peter . . . Her voice. She was talking. Answering.

"No, please, I don't want to talk about it."

"But you must. You must help us." That persistent voice. Why? Why?

"Why were you afraid of Carl, Nancy?"

She had to answer, if only to stop the questions.

She heard her voice, far away, trying to answer. . . . It was like watching herself in a play. . . . Scenes were taking shape.

Mother . . . the dinner . . . the last time she saw Mother . . .

Mother's face so troubled, looking at her, at Carl. "Where did you get that dress, Nancy?" She could tell Mother didn't like it.

The white wool dress. "Carl helped me pick it out. Do you like it?"

"Isn't it a bit . . . young?"

Mother left to make a call. Was it to Dr. Miles? Nancy hoped so. She wanted Mother to be happy. . . . Maybe she should go home with Mother. . . . Maybe she would stop feeling so tired. Did she say that to Carl?

Carl left the table. "Excuse me, dear." . . . Mother back before him . . .

"Nancy, you and I must talk tomorrow . . . when we're alone. I'll pick you up for breakfast."

Carl came back. . . .

And Mother . . . kissing her cheek . . . . "Good night, darling. I'll see you at eight." Mother getting in the rented car, waving good-bye, driving down the road . . .

Carl drove her back to school. "I'm afraid your mother doesn't approve of me yet, dear."

The call . . . "There's been an accident . . . Steering mechanism . . ."

Carl . . . "I'll take care of you, my little girl. . . ."

The funeral . . .

The wedding. A bride should wear white. She'd wear the white wool dress. It would do for just going to the Mayor's office.

But she couldn't wear it . . . grease stain at the shoulder. . . . "Carl, where could I have gotten grease on this dress? I only wore it to have dinner with Mother."

"I'll have it cleaned for you." His hand, familiar, patting her shoulder . . .

"No . . . no . . . no. . . ."

The voice. "What do you mean, Nancy?"

"I don't know. . . . I'm not sure. . . . I'm afraid. . . ."

"Afraid of Carl?"

"No . . . he is good to me. . . . I'm so tired . . . always so tired. . . . Drink your medicine. . . . You need it. . . . The children . . . Peter and Lisa . . . all right for a while. . . . Carl was good. . . . Please, Carl, close the door. . . . Please, Carl, I don't like that. . . . Don't touch me like that. . . . Leave me alone."

"How should he leave you alone, Nancy?"

"No . . . I don't want to talk about it. . . ."

"Was Carl good to the children?"

"He made them obey. . . . He wanted them to be good. . . . He made Peter afraid . . . and Lisa. . . . 'So my little girl has a little girl' . . ."

"Is that what Carl said?"

"Yes. He doesn't touch me anymore. . . . I'm glad. . . . But I mustn't have medicine after dinner . . . I get too tired. . . . There's something wrong. . . . I must get away. . . . The children . . . Get away . . ."

"From Carl?"

"I'm not sick. . . . Carl is sick. . . ."

"How is he sick, Nancy?"

"I don't know. . . ."

"Nancy, tell us about the day Lisa and Peter disappeared. What do you remember about that?"

"Carl is angry."

"Why is he angry?"

"The medicine . . . last night. . . . He saw me pour it out . . . got more . . . made me drink it. . . . So tired . . . so sleepy. . . . Lisa is crying . . . Carl . . . with her. . . . I must get up . . . must go to her. . . . Crying so hard. . . . Carl spanked her . . . said she wet the bed. . . . I have to take her away . . . in morning. . . . My birthday . . . I'll tell Carl. . . ."

"Tell him what?"

"He knows . . . he's beginning to know. . . ."

"Know what, Nancy?"

"I'm going away . . . take the children. . . . Have to go away. . . ."

"Didn't you love Carl, Nancy?"

"I should. He said, 'Happy birthday.' . . . Lisa so quiet. I promised her we'd make a birthday cake for me . . . She and Peter and I. . . . We'd go out and get candles and chocolate for it. It's a bad day . . . starting to rain. . . . Lisa may be getting sick. . . ."

"Did Carl go to school that day?"

"Yes. . . . He phoned. . . . I said we were going to shopping center . . . that after that I was going to stop at the doctor's to let him see Lisa. . . . I was worried. I said I'd go to the Mart at eleven . . . after the children's television program. . . ."

"What did Carl say when you told him you were worried about Lisa?"

"He said it was a bad day . . . if Lisa was getting a cold, he didn't want her out. I said I'd leave them in the car while I shopped. . . . They wanted to help with the cake. . . . They were excited about my birthday. They never had fun. . . . I shouldn't have let Carl be so strict . . . my fault. . . . I'll talk to doctor . . . have to ask doctor . . . about Lisa . . . about me. . . . Why am I always so tired? . . . Why do I take so much medicine? . . . Rob made children laugh. . . . They were so different around him. . . . Children should laugh. . . ."

"Were you in love with Rob, Nancy?"

"No. . . . I was in cage . . . had to get out . . . wanted to talk to someone. . . . Then Rob said what I said to him. . . . Wasn't like that . . . wasn't like that. . . ." Her voice began to rise.

Lendon's voice became soothing. "Then you took the children to the store at eleven."

"Yes. It's raining. . . . I told children to stay in car. . . . They said they would. . . . Such good little children . . . I left them in back seat of car. . . . Never saw them again . . . never . . . never . . ."

"Nancy, were there many cars in the lot?"

"No. . . . No one I knew in store. . . . So windy . . . cold . . . not many people. . . ."

"How long were you in the store?"

"Not long . . . ten minutes. . . . Couldn't find birthday candles. . . . Ten minutes. . . . Hurry back to car. . . . The children gone." Her voice was incredulous.

"What did you do, Nancy?"

"Don't know what to do. . . . Maybe they went to buy present for me. . . . Peter has money. . . . They wouldn't leave except for that. . . . They're so good. . . . That might make them leave. . . . Maybe in other store . . . the dime store. . . . Look in candy store . . . look in gift shop . . . hardware store . . . look back at car. . . . Look, look for children. . . ."

"Did you ask anyone if they'd been seen?"

"No. . . . Mustn't let Carl know. He'll be angry. . . . Don't want him to punish children. . . ."

"So you checked all the stores in the shopping center."

"Maybe they came looking for me . . . got lost. . . . Look in parking lot. . . . Maybe they couldn't find car again. . . . Begin calling them. . . . Frightened. . . . Someone said we'll call police and your husband. . . . I said, 'Don't tell my husband, please.' . . . Woman told about that at trial. . . . I just didn't want Carl to be angry. . . ."

"Why didn't you tell this at your trial?"

"Mustn't. . . . Lawyer said, Don't say Carl was angry. . . . Don't say you argued on phone. . . . Lisa didn't wet the bed . . . bed dry. . . ."

"What do you mean?"

"Bed dry. . . . Why did Carl hurt her? Why? Doesn't matter. . . .

Nothing matters. . . . Children gone. . . . Michael . . . Missy gone too. . . . Look for them . . . have to look for them. . . ."

"Tell us about looking for Michael and Missy, this morning."

"I must look at the lake. . . . Maybe they went to the lake. . . . Maybe they fell into the water. . . . Hurry, hurry. . . . Something is in the lake. . . . Something is underwater. . . ."

"What was underwater, Nancy?"

"Red, something red. . . . Maybe it's Missy's mitten . . . I must get it. . . . Water is so cold. . . . I can't reach it. . . . It's not a mitten. . . . It's cold, cold. . . ."

"What did you do?"

"Children aren't here. . . . Get out . . . get out of water. . . . So cold . . . the beach . . . I fell on the beach. . . . He was there . . . in the woods . . . watching me. . . . I saw him there . . . watching me. . . ."

Jed Coffin stood up. Ray jumped forward convulsively. Lendon held up a warning hand. "Who was there, Nancy?" he asked. "Tell us who was there."

"A man . . . I know him. . . . It was . . . it was . . . Rob Legler. . . . Rob Legler was there. . . . He was hiding . . . looking at me." Her voice rose, fell; her eyelids fluttered open, then closed again slowly. Ray paled. Dorothy inhaled sharply. So the two cases were linked.

"The amytal's about worn off. She'll be coming to soon." Lendon stood up, grimacing against the cramped sensation in his knees and thighs.

"Doctor, may I speak with you and Jonathan outside?" Jed's voice was noncommittal.

"Stay with her, Ray," Lendon cautioned. "She'll probably wake up any minute."

In the dining room, Jed faced Lendon and Jonathan. "Doctor, how long is this to go on?" Jed's face was impenetrable.

"I don't think we should attempt to question Nancy any further."

"What have we gotten from all this other than the fact that she was afraid of her husband; that she obviously did not love him and that Rob Legler may have been at the lake this morning?"

Lendon stared. "Good God, didn't you hear what that girl was saying? Don't you know what you were listening to?"

"I only know that I haven't heard one thing that will help me discharge my responsibility to find the Eldredge children. I heard Nancy Eldredge blaming herself for her mother's death, which is natural in a case where a visit to a child in school results in a parent's death. Her reactions to her first husband sound pretty hysterical. She's trying to blame him for the fact that she wanted out of their marriage."

"What impression did you get of Carl Harmon?" Lendon asked quietly.

"One of those possessive guys who marries a younger girl and wants the upper hand. Hell, he isn't any different than half the men on the Cape. I can cite you examples of guys who won't let their wives handle a dime except for food money. I know one who won't let his wife drive the family car. Another never lets his wife go out at night by herself. This kind of thing is common all over the world. Maybe that's why that Women's Lib bunch have something to beef about."

"Chief, do you know what pedophilia is?" Lendon asked quietly.

Jonathan nodded. "That's what I've been thinking," he said.

Lendon didn't give Jed time to answer. "In laymen's terms, it's a sexual deviation involving sexual activity of any type with a child who has not yet reached puberty."

"How does that fit in here?"

"It doesn't . . . not completely. Nancy was eighteen when she married. But in appearance she could look quite childish. Chief, is there any way you can run a check on Carl Harmon's background?"

Jed Coffin looked incredulous. When he answered, his voice

was trembling with repressed fury. He pointed to the sleet that was beating a steady, sharp staccato against the window. "Doctor," he said, "do you see and hear that? Somewhere out there two kids are either wandering around freezing or they're in the hands of God knows what kind of kook and maybe they're dead. But it's my job to find them and find them now. We have one distinct lead to all this. That is that both Nancy Eldredge and a gasoline attendant have placed Rob Legler, a pretty unsavory character, in the immediate vicinity. That's the kind of information I can do something about." His voice bit off the words scornfully. "And you're asking me to waste my time running a check on a dead man to prove some cockeyed theory."

The telephone rang. Bernie Mills, who'd been standing unobtrusively in the room, hurried to answer it. Now they were talking about running a check on Nancy's first husband. Wait till he told this to Jean. He picked up the phone quickly. It was the station house. "Put the Chief on." Sergeant Poler at the desk spat the words.

Lendon and Jonathan watched while Chief Coffin listened, then asked quick, short questions. "How long ago? Where?"

The men looked at each other silently. Lendon realized he was praying—an inarticulate, fervent prayer that the message was not bad news about the children.

Jed slapped the receiver back into the cradle and turned to them. "Rob Legler checked into the Adams Port Motel right here in town around ten-thirty this morning. A car we believe he stole has just been smashed up on Route 6A, but he got away. He's probably heading for the mainland. We've got an all-out search for him and I'm going over to direct it. I'll leave Officer Mills here. We'll get that Legler bird, and when we do, I think we'll really have the answer to what happened to those kids."

After the door had closed behind the Chief, Jonathan spoke to Lendon. "What do you make of this so far?" he asked.

Lendon waited a long minute before answering. *I am too close to this,* he thought. *I see Priscilla at that phone . . . calling me. Carl Harmon left the table after her. Where did he go? Did he overhear what Priscilla said to me? Nancy said her dress was smeared with grease. Hadn't she been saying in effect that she believed Carl's hand must have been smeared and when he put his hand on her shoulder, her dress got dirty? Hadn't she been trying to say that she believed Carl Harmon might have done something to Priscilla's car?* Lendon saw a violent pattern forming. But what purpose would this knowledge serve with Carl Harmon in his grave?

Jonathan said, "If your mind is running in the same direction as mine, going back to the disappearance of the Harmon children won't help us. You're thinking of the father."

"Yes," Lendon said.

"And since he is dead, we turn to Rob Legler, the man sent into the home by Carl Harmon and the one witness whose testimony convicted Nancy. How accurate is her statement about this morning under the amytal?"

Lendon shook his head. "I can't be sure. It's been known that even under sedation, some patients can resist and suppress. But I believe that she saw — or believes she saw — Rob Legler at Maushop Lake."

Jonathan said, "And at ten-thirty this morning he checked into a motel *alone.*"

Lendon nodded.

Without speaking again, the two men turned and looked out the window in the direction of the lake.

22

The five-o'clock television news gave little coverage to the Mid-eastern crisis, spiraling inflation, the automobile workers' threat-ened strike or the dismal standing of the New England Patriots. Most of the half hour broadcast was devoted to the disappearance of the Eldredge children and old film clips from the sensational Harmon murder case.

The pictures that had appeared in the *Cape Cod Community News* were reproduced. Special attention was focused on the one of Rob Legler leaving the San Francisco courthouse with Profes-sor Carl Harmon after Nancy Harmon's conviction for the willful murder of her children.

The commentator's voice was especially urgent when that picture was shown. "Rob Legler has been positively identified as being in the vicinity of the Eldredge home this morning. If you believe you have seen this man, please call this special number at once: KL five, three eight hundred. The lives of the Eldredge children may be at stake. If you believe you have any information which may lead to the person or persons responsible for the chil-dren's disappearance, we urge you to call this number: KL five, three eight hundred. Let me repeat it again: KL five, three eight hundred."

The Wigginses had closed their store when the power failed

and were home in time to catch the broadcast on their battery-operated television set.

"That fellow looks kind of familiar," Mrs. Wiggins said.

"You'd say that anyhow," her husband snorted.

"No . . . not really. There's something about him . . . the way he bends forward . . . Certainly is nothing to look at."

Jack Wiggins stared at his wife. "I was just thinking he's the type that might turn a young girl's head."

"Him? Oh, you mean the young one. I'm talking about the other fellow—the professor."

Jack looked at his wife condescendingly. "This is why I say women don't make good witnesses and never should be jurors. Nobody's talking about that Professor Harmon. He committed suicide. They're talking about the Legler fellow."

Mrs. Wiggins bit her lip. "I see. Well, guess you're right. It's just . . . oh, well . . ."

Her husband got up heavily. "When'll dinner be ready?"

"Oh, not long. But it's hard to worry about food when you think about little Michael and Missy . . . God knows where. . . . You think you just want to help them. I don't care what they say about Nancy Eldredge. She never came in the store much, but when she did, I liked to watch her with her kids. She had such a nice way with them—never upset, never cranky, the way half these young mothers are. It makes our little annoyances so unimportant, you know."

"What little annoyances do we have?" His tone was sharply suspicious.

"Well . . ." Mrs. Wiggins bit her lip. They'd had so much trouble with shoplifters this past summer. Jack got so upset even discussing it. That was why, all day, it just hadn't seemed worthwhile to tell him that she was absolutely certain that Mr. Parrish had stolen a large can of baby powder from the shelf this morning.

23

The five o'clock news was on in a modest home down the block from St. Francis Xavier Church in Hyannis Port. The family of Patrick Keeney was about to start dinner. All eyes were glued on the small portable set in the crowded junior-size dining room.

Ellen Keeney shook her head as the picture of Michael and Missy Eldredge filled the screen. Involuntarily, she glanced at her own children—Neil and Jimmy, Deirdre and Kit . . . one . . . two. . . . three . . . four. Whenever she took them to the beach, that was the way it was. She never stopped counting heads. *God, don't let anything happen to them, ever, please.* That was her prayer.

Ellen was a daily communicant at St. Francis Church and usually went to the same Mass as Mrs. Rose Kennedy. She remembered the days after the President and then Bobby were killed when Mrs. Kennedy would come into the church, her face lined with grief but still serene and composed. Ellen never watched her during Mass. Poor lady, she had a right to some privacy somewhere. Often Mrs. Kennedy would smile and nod and sometimes say, "Good morning" if they happened to walk out after Mass at the same moment. *How does she stand it?* Ellen wondered. *How can she stand it?* Now she was thinking the same thing. *How can Nancy Eldredge stand it? . . . especially when you think that it happened to her before.*

The commentator was talking about the article in the *Community News*—that the police were trying to track down the author. His words barely registered on Ellen's mind as she decided that Nancy was not responsible for the death of her children. It simply wasn't possible. No mother murdered her flesh and blood. She saw Pat looking at her and smiled at him faintly—a communication that said, *We are blessed, my dear; we are blessed.*

"He got awful fat," Neil said.

Startled, Ellen stared at her oldest child. At seven, Neil worried her. He was so daring, so unpredictable. He had Pat's dark-blond hair and gray eyes. He was small for his age, and she knew that worried him a little, but from time to time, she reassured him. "Daddy's tall and your Uncle John's tall, and someday you will be too." Still, Neil did look younger than anyone else in his class.

"Who got fat, dear?" she asked absently, turning her back to gaze at the screen.

"That man, the one in front. He's the one who gave me the dollar to ask for his mail at the post office last month. Remember, I showed you the note he wrote when you wouldn't believe me."

Ellen and Pat stared at the screen. They were looking at the picture of Rob Legler following Professor Carl Harmon out of the courtroom.

"Neil, you're mistaken. That man has been dead for a long time."

Neil looked aggrieved. "See. You never believe me. But when you kept asking me where I got that dollar and I told you, you didn't believe me either. He's a lot fatter and his hair's all gone, but when he leaned out of the station wagon, he had his head kind of pulled down on his neck like that man."

The anchorman was saying, ". . . any piece of information, no matter how irrelevant you may consider it."

Pat scowled.

"Why do you look mad, Daddy?" five-year-old Deirdre asked anxiously.

His face cleared. Neil had said, "like that man." "I guess because sometimes I realize how hard it is to raise a bunch like you," he answered, running his hand through her short curly hair, grateful that she was here within his touch. "Turn off the television, Neil," he ordered his son. "Now, children, before we say grace, we will pray that God sends the Eldredge children safely home."

Through the prayer that followed, Ellen's mind was far away. They had pleaded for any information, no matter how irrelevant it seemed, and Neil had gotten that dollar tip to pick up a letter at General Delivery. She remembered the day exactly: Wednesday, four weeks ago. She remembered the date because there was a parents' meeting at school that night and she was annoyed that Neil was late for the early dinner. Suddenly she remembered something.

"Neil, by any chance, do you still have the note the man gave you to show the post office?" she asked. "Didn't I see you put it in your bank with the dollar?"

"Yes, I saved it."

"Will you get it, please?" she asked him. "I want to see the name on it."

Pat was studying her. When Neil left, he spoke over the heads of the other children. "Don't tell me you put any stock . . ."

She suddenly felt ridiculous. "Oh, eat up, dear. I guess I just have a case of nerves. It's people like me who are always wasting policemen's time. Kit, pass me your plate. I'll cut up the end piece of the meat loaf just the way you like it."

24

It was all going so badly. Nothing was working as he'd expected. That foolish woman coming here and then the little girl; having to wait till she woke up, if she woke up, so that he could feel her twisting and pulling from him. Then the boy squirming away from him, hiding. He'd have to find him.

Courtney had a feeling of everything slipping away from him. His sense of pleasure and expectation had changed to disappointment and resentment. He wasn't perspiring anymore, but the heavy sweat still clung to his clothes and made them unpleasantly sticky against his body. The thought of the boy's big blue eyes, so like Nancy's, didn't give him anticipatory pleasure.

The boy was a threat. If he escaped, it would be the end. Better to finish with them both; better to do what he'd done before. In an instant he could remove the threat—seal off air so that lips and nostrils and eyes were covered—and then in a few hours— when the tide was high toss their bodies into the churning surf. No one would know. Then he'd be here safe again with nothing to threaten him; here to enjoy her torment.

And tomorrow night, with all the threat gone, he'd drive to the mainland. He'd go around dusk, and probably some little girl would be walking alone and he'd tell her he was the new teacher. . . . It always worked.

His decision made, he felt better. Now all he wanted was to be finished with this threat. That child, recalcitrant like Nancy . . . troublesome . . . ungrateful. . . . wanting to escape . . . he would find him. He'd tie him and then get the thin sheets of velvety plastic. He'd made sure to have a brand that Nancy could have bought at Lowery's. Then he'd seal it on the boy first, because the boy was so troublesome. And then . . . the little girl . . . right away too. It was too dangerous to even keep her.

The sense of danger always heightened his perception. Like last time. He hadn't really known what he would do when he had slipped across the campus to the shopping center. He'd only known that he couldn't let Nancy take Lisa to the doctor. He'd been there before she arrived, parked on that little supply road between the shopping center and the campus. He'd seen her drive in, speak to the children, go into the store. No cars nearby. Not a soul around. In a moment he'd known what to do.

The children had been so obedient. They'd looked startled and frightened when he opened the car door, but when he said, "Now, quickly—we're going to play a game on Mommy for her birthday," they'd gotten into the trunk and in an instant it was over. The plastic bags slipped over their heads, twisted tight, his hands holding them till they stopped squirming; the trunk shut and he back in school. Less than eight minutes gone in all; the students intent on their lab experiments, no one had missed him. A roomful of witnesses to testify to his presence if need be. That night he'd simply driven the car to the beach and dumped the bodies into the ocean. Opportunity seized, danger averted that day seven years ago, and now danger to be averted again. "Michael, come out, Michael. I'll take you home to your mother."

He was still in the kitchen. Holding the hurricane lamp up, he looked around. There was no place to hide here. The cupboards were all high. But finding the boy in this dark, cavernous house with only this lamp to see by would be infinitely difficult. It would take hours, and where should he begin?

"Michael, don't you want to go home to your mother?" he called again. "She didn't go to God . . . she's all better . . . she wants to see you."

Should he try the third floor and look in those bedrooms first? he wondered.

But the boy would probably have tried to get to this outside door. He was smart. He wouldn't have stayed upstairs. Would he have gone to the front door? Better to look there.

He started into the little hall, then thought of the small back parlor. If the boy had tried the kitchen and heard him coming, that would be the logical place to hide.

He walked to the doorway of the room. Was that breathing he was hearing, or only the wind sighing against the house? He walked a few steps farther, into the room, holding the kerosene lamp high above his head. His eyes darted, picking objects out of the gloom. He was about to turn around when he swung the lamp to his right.

Staring at what he was seeing, he let out a high-pitched, hysterical whinny. The shadow of a small figure huddled behind the couch was silhouetted like a giant crouched rabbit across the faded oak floor. "I found you, Michael," he cried, still giggling, "and this time you won't get away."

25

The power failure began as John Kragopoulos turned off Route 6A onto the road that led to The Lookout. Instinctively, he pressed the button under his foot to turn on the bright headlights. Vision was still poor, and he drove carefully, feeling the slick road under the tires and the tendency of the car to skid at the turns.

He wondered how he could possibly justify looking through that cavernous house for a small lighter. Mr. Parrish could reasonably suggest that he return in the morning or offer to search for it himself and give it to Dorothy if it was found.

John decided he would go to the door with his flashlight. He'd say that he was quite sure he remembered hearing something drop when he was bending over the telescope. He had meant to check to see if something had slipped out of his pocket. That was reasonable. It was the fourth-floor apartment that he wanted to see anyhow.

The hilly ascent to The Lookout was treacherous. At the last bend in the road, the front end of the car swayed precariously. John gripped the wheel as the tires grabbed and held the road. He had been within inches of veering onto the sloping embankment and would surely have hit the massive oak tree less than six feet away. A few minutes later, he turned the car into the back driveway of The Lookout, rejecting the alternative of pulling into the comparative shelter of the garage as Dorothy had done. He wanted to be casual, open. If anything his manner should be a bit irritated as though he were being inconvenienced too. He would say that since he had discovered his loss at dinner and was still in town, he'd decided to come right back rather than phone.

As he got out of the car, he was struck by the foreboding blackness of the big house. Even the top floor was completely dark. Surely the man had hurricane lamps. Power blackouts on the Cape in bad storms couldn't be unusual. Suppose Parrish had fallen asleep and didn't realize the electricity had failed? Suppose—just suppose—there'd been a woman visiting him who had not wanted to be seen. It was the first time the possibility had occurred to John.

Suddenly feeling foolish, he debated about getting back into the car. The sleet stung his face. The wind whipped it under the collar and sleeves of his coat, and the warm satisfaction of the dinner was dispelled. He realized he was chilled and tired and had a long, difficult drive ahead of him. He would look like a fool with his contrived story. Why hadn't he thought about the possibility that Parrish had a visitor who would be embarrassed at being seen? John decided he was a fool, a suspicious idiot. He and Dorothy had probably interrupted a liaison and nothing more. He'd get away from here before he made a further nuisance of himself.

He was about to get behind the wheel when he saw a glimmer of light from the far-left kitchen window. It moved swiftly, and a few seconds later he could see it reflected in the windows to the right of the kitchen door. Someone was walking around the kitchen with a lamp.

Carefully John closed the car door so that it made no slamming sound, only a soft click. Gripping the flashlight, he edged across the driveway to the kitchen window and peered in. The light seemed to be coming from the hall now. Mentally, he reviewed the layout of the house. The back staircase was reached through that hall, and so was the small parlor on the other side. Sheltering against the weathered shingles, he moved quickly along the back of the house, past the kitchen door, to the windows that should be those of the small parlor. The glow from the lamp was muted, but as he watched it grew stronger. He shrank back as the lamp became visible, held by an outstretched arm. He could see Courtney Parrish now. The man was searching for something . . . for what? He was calling to someone. John strained to hear. The wind smothered sound, but he could make out the name "Michael." Parrish was calling, "Michael!"

John felt chilling fear race along his spinal column. He had been right. The man was a maniac, and those children were somewhere in the house. The lamp he was arching in circles was a spotlight that illuminated the solid thickness of Parrish's bulk. John felt totally inadequate, aware that he was no physical match for this man. He had only the flashlight as a weapon. Should he go for help? Was it possible Michael had gotten away from Parrish? But if Parrish found him, even a few minutes might make a difference.

Then, before his horrified eyes, John saw Parrish swing the lamp over to the right and reach behind the couch to pull out a small figure who tried desperately to escape. Parrish put down the lamp and, as John watched, closed both hands around the child's throat.

Acting as instinctively as he had when he'd been on combat duty in World War II, John pulled his arm back and smashed the window with his flashlight. As Courtney Parrish spun around, John reached his hand in and forced the lock open. With superhuman strength, he pushed the window up and vaulted over the sill into the room. He dropped the flashlight as his feet hit the floor, and Parrish grabbed for it. Still holding the hurricane lamp in his left hand, Parrish raised the flashlight in his right hand, holding it over his head like a weapon.

There was no way to escape the inevitable blow. But John ducked and weaved back against the wall for time. Shouting, "Run away, Michael. . . . Call help," he managed to kick the kerosene lamp from Parrish's hand an instant before the flashlight crashed down on his skull.

26

It had been a mistake to ditch the car. It had been an act of sheer, stupid panic. Rob believed in making your own luck. Today he had made every blunder in the book. When he saw Nancy at the lake, he should have gotten the hell off Cape Cod. Instead, he'd figured that she might be on a trip or stoned and all he had to do was lie low for a day and then go see her and her husband and get some money. Now he'd made a point of placing himself in the vicinity, and her kids were missing.

Rob had never really believed that Nancy had anything to do with the other kids' disappearance; but now, who could know? Maybe she did go haywire, just as Harmon used to tell him.

When he left the car, Rob had headed south toward the main expressway that ran through the center of the Cape. But when a police car whipped past him, he'd doubled back. Even if he could hitch a ride, the odds were they'd have a roadblock at the bridge. It would be better to head toward the bay. There had to be plenty of closed-up summer cottages there. He'd break into one of them and hole up for a while. Most of them probably had some staples left in the kitchen, and he was getting hungry. Then in a couple of days, when the heat was off, he'd find a truck, hide in the back and get off this damned island.

He shivered as he hurried down the narrow, darkened roads.

One good thing: in this shit weather, there wasn't any danger of running into people out walking. Hardly any cars on the road, either.

But when he rounded a bend in the road, Rob barely had time to jump back into thick hedges to escape being revealed by the headlights of an approaching car. Breathing harshly, he waited till the automobile had screeched past him. Christ. Another cop car. The place was swarming with them. He'd have to get off the road. It couldn't be more than a couple of blocks to the beach now. Moving swiftly along the row of hedges, Rob headed toward the clump of woods that edged the back of the houses near him. Less chance of being spotted there, even if it took longer to wind through backyards.

Suppose Nancy had seen him at the lake? She did look in his direction . . . but maybe not. He'd deny he was there, of course. She was in no state to be a witness about seeing him. Nobody else had. He was sure of that. Except . . . the driver of that station wagon. Probably a local guy . . . Massachusetts plates . . . 8X642. . . . How did he remember that? The reverse. . . . oh, sure . . . 2-4-6-8. He'd noticed that. If Rob did get caught, he could tell the cops about that station wagon. He'd seen it backing out of the dirt road leading from the Eldredge property, and that must have been just around the time the kids disappeared.

But on the other hand, suppose that station wagon was a regular delivery car that they already knew about? Rob hadn't seen the driver at all; hadn't paid attention, really . . . just noticed he was a big, fat guy. If he did get caught and told about the station wagon, he'd only nail himself as having been Johnny-on-the-spot at the Eldredge house.

No, he wouldn't admit anything if they got him. He'd say he had been planning to visit Nancy. Then he had seen his picture in that story about the Harmon case and decided to get away. The decision made, Rob felt better. Now if he could just get to the beach and into a cottage . . .

He hurried, careful to stay well in the shadows of the stark trees; stumbled; swore softly and recovered his balance. This sleet was making the whole damn place as slippery as a skating rink. But he couldn't have much farther to go. He had to get indoors somewhere, or someone would be sure to spot him. Steadying himself against the ice-crusted trees, he tried to move faster.

27

Thurston Givens sat quietly in his glassed-in back porch, watching the storm in the near dark. An octogenarian, he'd always found nor'easters fascinating and knew that he wouldn't be likely to see them for too many more years. The radio was on very low, and he'd just heard the latest bulletin about the Eldredge children. There was still no trace of them.

Now Thurston sat staring out toward the back, wondering why young people had to know so much misery. His only child had died at five from flu during the epidemic of 1917.

A retired realtor, Thurston knew Ray Eldredge well. He'd been a friend of Ray's father and grandfather, too. Ray was a fine fellow, the kind of man the Cape needed. He was a go-getter and a good realtor— not the kind out to turn a fast buck and the public be damned. Damn shame if anything happened to those little children of his. Nancy certainly didn't strike Thurston as the type to get mixed up with murdering anyone. There had to be a better answer than that.

He was drifting into a kind of reverie when some movement in the woods caught his attention. He leaned forward and peered through narrowed eyes. There was someone out there, sliding along, obviously trying to stay hidden. Nobody up to any good was in those woods in this kind of weather, and there'd been a lot of robberies on the Cape, and particularly in this area.

Thurston reached for the phone. He dialed Police Headquarters. Chief Coffin was an old friend, but, of course, the Chief probably wasn't there. He must be out on the Eldredge case.

The phone was answered at the other end, and a voice said, "Adams Port Police Headquarters. Sergeant Poler—"

Thurston interrupted impatiently. "Thurston Givens here," he said crisply. "I want you fellows to know there's a prowler in the woods behind my place and he's heading towards the bay."

28

Nancy sat upright on the couch, staring straight ahead. Ray had lighted the fire, and the flames were beginning to lick at the thick twigs and broken pieces of branches. Yesterday. It was just yesterday, wasn't it? She and Michael had been raking the front lawn.

"This is the last time we'll have this job this winter, Mike," she'd said. "I guess just about all the leaves are down now."

He'd nodded soberly. Then, without her telling him, he'd picked out the biggest chunks of branch and thick twigs from the pile of leaves. "These are good for fires," he commented. He'd dropped the iron rake, and it had fallen with the metal prongs facing upward. But when Missy came running from the driveway, he'd quickly turned over the rake. With an apologetic half-smile he'd said, "Daddy always says it's dangerous to leave a rake like that."

He was so protective of Missy. He was so good. He was so like Ray. Nancy realized that in some incredible way there was comfort in knowing that Mike was with Missy. If there was any way to do it, he'd take care of her. He was such a resourceful little kid. If they were outside somewhere now, he'd make sure that her jacket was zipped up. He'd try to cover her. He'd . . .

"Oh, God."

She didn't know she'd spoken aloud until Ray looked up startled. He was sitting in his big chair. His face looked so strained. He seemed to know that she didn't want him to touch her now—that she needed to assimilate and evaluate. She must not believe that the children were dead. They could not be dead. But they must be found before anything happened.

Dorothy was watching her too. Dorothy, who suddenly looked so much older and so lost. She had taken Dorothy's affection and love without giving in return. She had held Dorothy at arm's length, made it clear that Dorothy was not to intrude on their closed family circle. She didn't want the children to have a grandmother substitute. She didn't want anyone to replace Mother.

I have been selfish, Nancy thought. *I have not seen her need.* How odd that it was so clear now. How odd to even think about that now when they were sitting here, so helpless, so powerless. Then why was something reassuring her? Why was she feeling some tiny lick of hope? What was the source of her comfort?

"Rob Legler," she said. "I told you that I saw Rob Legler at the lake this morning."

"Yes," Ray said.

"Is it possible I was dreaming? Does the doctor believe that I saw him—that I was telling the truth?"

Ray considered, then decided to be honest. There was a strength in Nancy, a directness that wouldn't tolerate evasion.

"I believe that the doctor feels that you gave an exact account of what happened. And Nancy, you should know, Rob Legler has definitely been seen near here both last night and this morning."

"Rob Legler would not hurt the children." Nancy's voice was matter-of-fact, flatly positive. That was her area of comfort. "If he took them, if he was responsible, he wouldn't hurt them. I know it."

Lendon came back into the room, Jonathan close behind him. Jonathan realized that he inadvertently looked for Dorothy first. Her hands were dug into her pockets. He suspected they were

gripped into fists. She had always struck him as a remarkably efficient, self-sufficient person—traits that he admired without finding
them necessarily endearing in a woman.

When Jonathan was honest with himself, he realized that an
essential part of his relationship with Emily had been his constant
awareness of her need for him. She never could unscrew the cap
from a jar or find her car keys or balance her checking account. He
had basked in his role as the indulgent, able, constant fixer, doer,
solver. It had taken the past two years to make him begin to realize
that he'd never understood the steel shaft of strength at the core
of Emily's femininity: the way she'd accepted the doctor's verdict
with only a sympathetic glance at him; the way she'd never once
admitted to pain. Now, seeing Dorothy with her mute anguish so
tangible, he ached somehow to comfort her.

He was diverted by a question from Ray. "What was the phone
call?"

"Chief Coffin went out," Jonathan said evasively.

"It's all right. Nancy knows that Rob Legler has been seen near
here."

"That's why the Chief left. Legler was chased and left a car he'd
stolen two miles down on 6A. But don't worry, he won't get far on
foot in this weather."

"How do you feel, Nancy?" Lendon studied her closely. She
was more composed than he'd expected.

"I'm all right. I talked a lot about Carl, didn't I?"

"Yes."

"There was something I was trying to remember; something
important I wanted to tell you."

Lendon kept his voice matter-of-fact. "Several times you said, 'I
don't believe . . . I don't believe. . . .' Do you know why you would
say that?"

Nancy shook her head. "No." She got up and walked restlessly to the window. "It's so dark, it would be hard to find anything or anybody now."

Movement was desirable. She wanted to try to clear her head to be able to think. She looked down, realizing for the first time that she was still wearing the fluffy woolen robe. "I'm going to change," she said. "I want to get dressed."

"Do you . . . ?" Dorothy bit her lip. She'd been about to ask if Nancy wanted her to go upstairs with her.

"I'll be all right," Nancy said gently. They were going to find Rob Legler. She was sure of it. When they did, she wanted to be dressed. She wanted to go to him wherever they took him. She wanted to say, "Rob, I know you wouldn't hurt the children. Do you want money? What do you need? Tell me where they are and we'll give you anything."

Upstairs in the bedroom, she took off her robe. Mechanically, she walked over to the closet and hung it up. For an instant, she felt lightheaded and leaned her forehead against the coolness of the wall. The bedroom door opened, and she heard Ray cry, "Nancy!" His voice was startled as he hurried over to her, turned her to him and put his arms around her. She felt the scratchy warmth of his sports shirt against her skin and the growing intensity of his grasp.

"I'm all right," she said. "Really. . . ."

"Nancy!" He tilted her head up. His mouth closed over hers. As her lips parted, she arched her body against his.

It had been like this from the beginning. From that first night when he'd come to dinner and afterward they'd walked down to the lake. It had been chilly, and she'd shivered. His coat was open, and he'd laughed and pulled her against him, wrapping the coat around so that it covered her too. When he'd kissed her that first time, it had been so inevitable. She'd wanted him so much, right from the beginning. Not like Carl. . . . Poor Carl . . . she'd only tolerated him; felt guilty about not wanting him, and after Lisa was born, he had never again . . . not like a husband . . . Had he sensed her revulsion? She'd always wondered. It was part of her guilt.

"I love you." She didn't know she'd said it—words said so often, words she murmured to Ray even in her sleep.

"I love you too. Oh, Nancy. It must have been so bad for you. I thought I understood, but I didn't. . . ."

"Ray, will we get the children back?" Her voice shook, and she felt her whole body begin to tremble.

His arms tightened. "I don't know, darling. I don't know. But remember this: No matter what happens, we have each other. Nothing can change that. They've just come by for the Chief. They have Rob Legler at the station house. Dr. Miles went with them, and Jonathan and I are going over too."

"I want to go. Maybe he'll tell me . . ."

"No. Jonathan has an idea, and I think it could work. We've got to find out. Maybe Rob has an accomplice who has the children. If he sees you, he might refuse to say anything, especially if he was involved last time."

"Ray . . ." Nancy heard the despair in her voice.

"Darling, hang on. Just a little while longer. Take a hot shower and get dressed. Dorothy will stay with you. She's fixing a sandwich for you now. I'll be back as soon as I can." For an instant he buried his lips in her hair, then was gone.

Mechanically, Nancy walked into the bathroom off the bedroom. She turned on the water in the shower stall, then looked into the mirror over the washbasin. The face she saw looking back at her was pale and drawn, the eyes heavy and clouded. It was the way she had looked all those years with Carl, like the pictures of her in that article.

Quickly she turned away and, twisting her hair into a knot, stepped into the shower. The warm needle spray struck her body, making a steady assault against the rigid tension of her muscles. It felt good. Gratefully she lifted her face to the spray. A shower felt so clean.

She never, never took a tub bath anymore—not since the years with Carl. She didn't think about those baths anymore. A vivid shaft of recollection came as the water splashed against her face. The tub . . . Carl's insistence on bathing her . . . the way he had touched and examined her. Once when she'd tried to push him away, he'd slipped and his face had gone under the water. He'd been so startled that for a moment he couldn't pull up. When he did, he'd begun sputtering and trembling and coughing. He'd been so angry . . . but mostly so frightened. It had terrified him to have his face covered by the water.

That was it. That was what she had tried to remember: that secret fear of water. . . .

Oh, God. Nancy swayed against the side of the shower stall. She felt nausea rack her stomach and throat, stumbled out of the shower and began retching uncontrollably.

Minutes passed. She clung to the sides of the commode, unable to stem the violent waves of illness. Then, even when the vomiting finally stopped, icy chills still shuddered through her body.

29

"Ray, don't count on too much," Jonathan warned.

Ray ignored him. Through the streaked windowpane, he could see the station house. The glow from the gas lamps gave it the look of another century. Quickly parking the car, Ray threw open the door and darted across the macadam into the station. From behind he could hear Jonathan puffing as he tried to keep pace.

The desk sergeant looked surprised. "Didn't expect to see you here tonight, Mr. Eldredge. I'm sure sorry about the kids. . . ."

Ray nodded impatiently. "Where are they questioning Rob Legler?"

The sergeant looked alarmed. "You can't have anything to do with that, Mr. Eldredge."

"The hell I can't," Ray said evenly. "Go in and tell the Chief that I have to see him now."

The sergeant's protest died on his lips. He turned to a policeman who was coming down the corridor. "Tell the Chief that Ray Eldredge wants to see him," he snapped.

Ray turned to Jonathan. With the trace of a wan smile, he said, "Suddenly this seems like a farfetched, crazy idea."

"It isn't," Jonathan replied quietly.

Ray glanced around the room and realized for the first time that two people were sitting on a small bench near the door. They were just about as old as he and Nancy—a nice-looking couple. He wondered abstractedly what they were doing here. The guy looked embarrassed, the woman determined. What would bring anyone out on a night like this? Was it possible they had had a fight and she was pressing charges? The idea was wildly funny. Somewhere outside this room, outside this whole incredible day, people were home with their families; cooking dinner in candlelight, telling kids not to be scared of the dark, making love . . . having fights. . . .

He realized that the woman was staring at him. She started to get up, but the husband pulled her down. Quickly, Ray turned his back to her. The last thing in the world he wanted or needed was sympathy.

Footsteps hurried down the corridor. Chief Coffin rushed into the room. "What is it, Ray? Have you heard anything?"

Jonathan answered. "You have Rob Legler here?"

"Yes. We're questioning him. Dr. Miles is with me. Legler's asking for a lawyer. Won't answer any questions."

"I thought as much. That's why we're here." In a low voice, Jonathan outlined his plan.

Chief Coffin shook his head. "Won't work. This guy's a cool one. There's no way you'll get him to place himself at the Eldredge house this morning."

"Well, let us try. Can't you see how important time is? If he had an accomplice who has the children now, that person may panic. God knows what he might do."

"Well . . . come in here. Talk to him. But don't count on anything." With a jerk of his head, the Chief nodded to a room halfway down the corridor. As Ray and Jonathan started to follow him, the woman got up from the bench.

"Chief Coffin." Her voice was hesitant. "Could I speak to you for just a minute?"

The Chief looked at her appraisingly. "Is it important?"

"Well, probably not. It's just that I felt I wouldn't have any peace unless . . . It's something my little boy . . ."

The Chief visibly lost interest. "Just sit down please, ma'am. I'll be back with you as soon as I can."

Ellen Keeney sank down on the bench as she watched the three men leave. The sergeant at the desk sensed her disappointment. "Are you sure I can't help you, ma'am?" he asked.

But Ellen didn't trust the sergeant. When she and Pat had first come in, they had tried to tell him that they thought their little boy might know something about the Eldredge case. The sergeant had looked pained. "Lady, do you know how many calls we've had today? Since the wire services got hold of this, we've had nothing but calls. Some jerk from Tucson phoned to say he thought he saw the kids in a playground across the street from his apartment this morning. No way they could have gotten there, even in a supersonic plane. So just take a seat. The Chief'll talk to you when he can."

Pat said, "Ellen, I think we should go home. We're only in the way here."

Ellen shook her head. She opened her pocketbook and took out the note the stranger had given Neil when he had sent him in for the mail. She had attached the note to her own scribblings about everything Neil had told her. She knew the exact time he had gone in for the letter. She had carefully written down his description of the man; his exact words when he'd said the man looked like the picture on television of Nancy Harmon's first husband; the kind of car the man was driving—"a real old station wagon just like Gramp's"—that sounded like a Ford. Last, Neil had said that the man had a fishing permit for Adams Port on his windshield.

Ellen was determined to sit here until she got a chance to tell her story. Pat looked so tired. Reaching over, she patted his hand. "Bear with me, dear," she whispered. "I suppose it doesn't mean anything, but something is making me wait. The Chief did say he'd talk to me soon."

The door to the station house opened. A middle-aged couple came in. The man looked thoroughly annoyed; the woman was visibly nervous. The desk sergeant greeted them. "Hi, Mr. Wiggins . . . Miz Wiggins. Anything wrong?"

"You won't believe it," Wiggins snapped. "On a night like this, my wife wants to report that somebody pilfered a can of baby powder from the store this morning."

"Baby powder?" The sergeant's voice ranged upward in astonishment.

Mrs. Wiggins looked more upset. "I don't care how stupid it sounds. I want to see Chief Coffin."

"He'll be coming out soon. These people are waiting for him too. Just sit down, won't you?" He pointed to the bench at a right angle to the one where the Keeneys were waiting.

They came over, and as they sat down, the husband muttered angrily, "I still don't know why we're here."

Ellen's ready sympathy made her turn to the couple. She thought that maybe just talking to someone would help the other woman to get over her nervousness. "We don't really know why we're here either," she said. "But isn't it an awful thing about those missing children. . . ."

Fifty feet away in the office down the corridor, Rob Legler stared through narrowed, hostile eyes at Ray Eldredge. The guy had class, he decided. Nancy had certainly done a lot better this time. That Carl Harmon had been some creep. Fear knotted Rob's stomach. The Eldredge kids hadn't been found. If anything had happened to them, they might try to pin something on him. But nobody had seen him near the Eldredge house . . . nobody except that fat slob who'd been in the old station wagon. Suppose that guy had been a deliveryman or something and called the cops? Suppose he could identify Rob as being around the Eldredge house this morning? What excuse did he have for being there? No one would believe that he had sneaked into the country just to say hello to Nancy.

Mentally, Rob darted around for a story. There was none that made sense. He'd just keep his mouth shut until he got a lawyer— and maybe after that too. The older guy was talking to him.

"You are in a very serious situation," Jonathan was saying. "You are a deserter who has been taken into custody. Shall I remind you of the penalty the law holds for deserters? Your situation is far more serious than that of a man who left the country to avoid conscription. You were a member of the armed forces. No matter what has happened to the Eldredge children or how guilty or innocent you are in their disappearance, you stand right now to spend the better part of the next ten or twenty years in prison."

"We'll see about that," Rob muttered. But he knew Jonathan was right. *Christ!*

"But, of course, even the desertion charge isn't nearly so serious as a murder charge. . . ."

"I never murdered anyone," Rob snarled, jumping up from his chair.

"Sit down," Chief Coffin ordered.

Ray stood up and leaned across the table until his eyes were on a level with Rob's. "I'm going to lay it out for you," he said evenly. "I think you're a bastard. For two cents, I'd kill you myself. Your testimony almost put my wife in a gas chamber seven years ago, and right now you may know something that could save my children's lives if it isn't already too late. Now, listen, bum, and listen hard. My wife doesn't believe that you could or would harm our children. I happen to respect that belief. But she saw you there this morning. So that means you've got to know something about what went on. Trying to stall and say you never got to our house won't help. We'll prove you were there. But if you level with us now, and we get our kids back, we won't prosecute a kidnapping charge. And Mr. Knowles, who happens to be one of the top lawyers in the country, will be your lawyer, to get you off with as light a sentence as possible on the desertion charges. He has pull—plenty of it. . . . Now, which is it, punk? Do you take the deal?" The veins bulged out in Ray's forehead. He moved forward until his eyes were inches away from Rob's. "Because if you don't . . . and if you know something . . . and if I find out that you could have helped us get our kids back and didn't . . . I don't care what jail they throw you in . . . I'll get to you and I'll kill you. Just remember that, you stinking bastard."

"Ray." Jonathan pulled him back forcibly.

Rob stared from face to face: The Chief . . . the doctor . . . Ray Eldredge . . . that Knowles guy, the lawyer. If he admitted being at the Eldredge house . . . but what good not to admit it? There was a witness. His instinct told him to take the offer that had been made. Rob knew when he had no cards left to play. At least by taking the offer, he had some leverage on the desertion business.

He shrugged and looked at Jonathan. "You'll defend me."

"Yes."

"I don't want any bum kidnapping rap."

"No one's trying to pin one on you," Jonathan said. "We want the truth—the simple truth, as you know it. And the deal's off unless we get it now."

Rob leaned back. He avoided looking at Ray. "Okay," he said. "This is how it started. My buddy up in Canada . . ."

They listened intently as he talked. Only occasionally did the Chief or Jonathan ask a question. Rob chose his words carefully when he said he was coming to ask Nancy for money. "See, I never believed she touched a hair on the head of those Harmon kids. She wasn't the type. But I got the word that they were trying to pin the rap on me out there and I'd better just answer questions and keep my opinions out of it. I felt kind of sorry for her; she was a scared kid in a big frame-up as far as I was concerned."

"A frame-up that was your direct responsibility," Ray said.

"Shut up, Ray," Chief Coffin said. "Get to this morning," he ordered Rob. "When did you arrive at the Eldredge home?"

"It was like a couple of minutes before ten," Rob said. "I had been driving real slow, looking for that dirt road my friend drew a picture of . . . and then I realized I'd missed it."

"How did you realize you missed it?"

"Well, this other car . . . I had to slow down for . . . Then I realized that the other car had come off that road, so I backed up."

"The other car?" Ray repeated. He jumped up. "*What* other car?"

The door of the interrogation room burst open. The sergeant hurried in. "Chief, I think it's real important you talk to the Wigginses and that other couple. I think they have something real important to tell you."

30

Finally Nancy was able to get up, wash her face and rinse her mouth. She mustn't let them see that she'd been sick. She mustn't talk about it. They'd think she was crazy. They wouldn't believe or understand. But if the unbelievable was possible . . . The children. Oh, God, not again, not like that; please, not again.

She rushed into the bedroom and grabbed underwear from the drawer, slacks and a heavy sweater from the closet. She had to go to the station house. She had to see Rob, tell him what she believed, beg him for the truth. What did it matter if everyone thought she was crazy?

With lightning speed, she dressed, stuffed her feet into sneakers, laced them with trembling fingers and hurried downstairs. Dorothy was waiting for her in the dining room. The table was set with sandwiches and a pot of tea.

"Nancy, sit down. . . . Just try to have something. . . ."

Nancy cut her off. "I have to see Rob Legler. There's something I have to ask him." She clenched her teeth together, having heard the hysteria rising in her voice. She must not be hysterical. She turned to Bernie Mills, who was standing in the doorway of the kitchen.

"Please call the station," she begged him. "Tell Chief Coffin I insist on coming over . . . that it has to do with the children."

"Nancy!" Dorothy grabbed her arm. "What are you saying?"

"That I must see Rob. Dorothy, call the station. No, I will."

Nancy ran over to the phone. She was just reaching for it when it rang. Bernie Mills hurried to take it, but she picked it up.

"Hello?" Her voice was quick and impatient.

Then she heard. So low it was a whisper. She had to strain to make out his words. "Mommy. Mommy, please come and get us. Help us, Mommy. Missy is sick. Come and get us. . . ."

"Michael . . . Michael!" she screamed. "Michael, where are you? Tell me where you are!"

"We're at . . ." Then his voice faded and the line went dead.

Frantically, she jiggled the phone. "Operator," she shrieked, "don't break the connection! Operator . . ." But it was too late. An instant later, the monotonous dull, buzzing dial tone whined in her ear.

"Nancy, what is it? Who was it?" Dorothy was at her side.

"It was Michael. Michael phoned. He said Missy is sick." Nancy could see doubt on Dorothy's face. "In God's name, don't you understand? That was Michael!"

Frantically, she jiggled the phone, then dialed the operator who broke into her perfunctory offer of help when she responded. "Can you tell me about the call that just came here? Who handled it? Where did it come from?"

"I'm sorry, ma'am. We have no way of knowing that. In fact, we're having a lot of trouble generally. Most of the phones in town are out because of the storm. What is the problem?"

"I've got to know where that call came from. I've got to know."

"There is no way we can trace the call once the connection is broken, ma'am."

Numbly, Nancy put down the receiver.

"Somebody may have broken that connection," she said. "Whoever has the children."

"Nancy, are you sure?"

"Mrs. Eldredge, you're kind of strung-up and upset."

Bernie Mills tried to make his voice soothing.

Nancy ignored him. "Dorothy, Michael said, 'We're at . . .' He knows where he is. He can't be far away. Don't you see that? And he says Missy's sick."

From far off, she was hearing something else. Lisa is sick. . . . She doesn't feel right. She had said that to Carl long ago.

"What is the number of the police station?" Nancy asked Bernie Mills. She pushed back the waves of weakness that were like clouds of fog inside her head. It would be so easy to lie down . . . to slip away. Right now someone was with Michael and Missy . . . someone who was hurting them . . . maybe was doing to them what had happened before. No . . . no . . . she had to find them. . . . She mustn't get sick. . . . She had to find them.

She grasped the edge of the table to steady herself. She said quietly, "You may think I'm hysterical, but I am telling you that was my son's voice. What is the number of the police station?"

"Call KL five, three eight hundred," Bernie said reluctantly. *She's really flipped*, he thought. And the Chief would have his head for not having gotten to the phone. She imagined it was the kid . . . but it could have been anybody, or even a crank.

The number rang once. A crisp voice said, "Adams Port Police Headquarters. Sergeant . . . speaking." Nancy started to say, "Chief Coffin" and realized that she was speaking into nothingness. Impatiently, she jiggled the phone. "It's dead," she said. "The phone is dead."

Bernie Mills took it from her. "It's dead, all right. I'm not surprised. Probably half the houses don't have phones by now. This is some storm."

"Take me to the police station. No, you go if the phone comes back on and Michael can call again . . . Please go to the police station, or is someone outside?"

"I don't think so. The television van went to the station house too."

"Then you go. We'll stay here. Tell them Michael phoned. Tell them to bring Rob Legler here. We've got to wait."

"I can't leave you."

"Nancy, how sure are you it was Michael?"

"I'm sure. Dorothy, please believe me. I'm sure. It was Michael. It was. Officer. Please. How far is the station in your car? . . . Five minutes. You'll be gone ten minutes in all. —But make them bring Rob Legler here. Please."

Bernie Mills thought carefully. The Chief had told him to stay here. But with the phone out, there wouldn't be messages. If he brought Nancy with him, the Chief might not like it. If he left and came right back, he'd be gone a total of ten minutes, and if that ever was the kid on the phone and he didn't report it. . . .

He considered asking Dorothy to drive to the station, then discarded the idea. The roads were too icy. She looked so upset that the odds were she'd crack up her car.

"I'll go," he said. "Stay right here."

He didn't take time to look for his coat, but ran out the back door to the patrol car.

Nancy said, "Dorothy, Michael knew where he was. He said, 'We're at . . .' What does that mean to you? If you're on a street or a road, you say, 'We're on Route 6A,' or 'we're on the beach,' or 'we're on the boat'; but if you're in a house or store, you know you say, 'We're at Dorothy's house'; or 'We're at Daddy's office.' Do you see what I mean? Oh, Dorothy, there must be some way to know. I keep going over things. There must be something . . . some way to know.

"And he said that Missy is sick. I almost didn't let her go out this morning. I thought about it. I thought about it. Was it too cold; was it too windy? But I hate to think about them being sick or to baby them about being sick, and I know why now. It was because of Carl and the way he examined them . . . and me. He was sick. I know that now. But that's why I let Missy out. It was damp and too cold for her. But I thought just half an hour. And it was because of that. And I got her red mittens, the ones with the smile faces, and I told her to be sure to keep them on because it was so cold. I remember thinking that for a change she had a matching pair. But she did lose one by the swing. Oh, God, Dorothy, if I hadn't let them out! If I had kept them in because she was getting sick . . . But I didn't want to think about that. . . . Dorothy!"

Nancy spun around at Dorothy's strangled cry. Dorothy's face was working convulsively. "What did you say?" she demanded. "What did you say . . . about the mittens?"

"I don't know. Do you mean—that she lost one—or that they matched? Dorothy, what do you mean? . . . What do you know?"

With a sob, Dorothy covered her face. "I know where they are. Oh God, I know . . . and I was so stupid. Oh, Nancy, what have I done? Oh, what have I done?" She reached into her pocket and pulled out the mitten. "It was there . . . this afternoon on the floor of the garage and I thought I'd kicked it out. And that awful man . . . I knew there was something about him; the way he smelled so sour . . . so evil . . . and that baby powder. Oh, my God!"

Nancy grabbed the mitten. "Dorothy, please help me. Where did you find that mitten?"

Dorothy sagged limply. "At The Lookout, when I was showing it today."

"The Lookout . . . where that Parrish man lives. I don't think I've ever seen him except from a distance. Oh, no!" In an instant of total clarity, Nancy saw truth and realized it might be too late. "Dorothy, I'm going to The Lookout. Now . . . the children are there. Maybe. Maybe I'll be in time. You go for Ray and the police. Tell them to come. Can I get into the house?"

Dorothy's shaking stopped. Her voice became as calm as Nancy's. Later—later, for the rest of her life—she could indulge in self-recrimination . . . but not this minute. "The kitchen door has a bolt. If he put it on, you can't get in. But the front door, the one on the bay side—he never uses it. I never gave him a key. This will open both locks." She dug into her pocket and came out with a set. "This one."

She did not question Nancy's decision to go alone. Together the women raced out the back door toward the cars. Dorothy let Nancy pull out first. She caught her breath as Nancy's car lurched, skidded and then righted itself.

It was almost impossible to see. The sleet had formed a thick ice shield against the window. Nancy rolled down her side window. Glancing out it, squinting against the pelting sleet, she raced the car down the road, across Route 6A and down the street that led to the cutoff for The Lookout.

As she started up the winding incline, the car began to slip. She floored the gas pedal and the front wheels skidded, twisting the car on the icy road. Nancy jammed on the brake. The car spun around. Too late, she tried to right it. A tree loomed ahead. She managed to yank the wheel in a half circle. The front end of the car pulled to the right and with a grinding crash hit the tree.

Nancy was thrown forward, then snapped back. The wheels were still spinning as she pushed open the door on the driver's side and stepped out into the pelting sleet. She hadn't put on a coat, but she barely felt the sleet go through her sweater and slacks as she tried to run up the precarious hill.

At the approach to the driveway, she slipped and fell. Ignoring the sharp pain in her knee, she ran toward the house. *Don't let me be too late. Please don't let me be too late.* Like clouds breaking before her vision, she could see herself staring down at the slabs at Lisa and Peter . . . their faces white and bloated from the water . . . the bits of the plastic bag still sticking to them. *Please,* she prayed. *Please!*

She got to the house and steadied herself against the shingles as she ran around it toward the front entrance. The key in her hand was wet and cold. She grasped it tightly. The house was completely dark except for the top floor. She could see a light coming through the shade on one of the windows. As she rounded the house, she could hear the harsh crashing sounds of the bay as the waves broke against the rocky shore. There was no beach—just piles of rock. The beach was over to the left.

She hadn't realized this property was so high. You could probably see the whole town from the back windows.

Her breath was coming in deep, sobbing gasps. Nancy felt her heart pounding. She couldn't breathe from running in the cold wind. Her numbed fingers fumbled with the key. *Let it turn; please, let it turn.* She felt resistance as the rusty lock grabbed at the key, then held it, and finally the lock turned and Nancy pushed open the door.

The house was dark—so terribly dark. She couldn't see. There was a musty smell, and it was so quiet here. The light had come from the top floor. That was where the apartment was. She'd have to find the stairs. She resisted the impulse to shriek Michael's name.

Dorothy had said something about two staircases in the foyer past the big front room. This was the front room. Uncertainly, Nancy started forward. In the pitch darkness, she reached her hands in front of her. She mustn't make noise; mustn't give warning. She tripped, fell forward and recovered herself by grabbing something. It was the arm of a couch or chair. She felt her way around it. If only she had matches. She strained to hear. . . . Had she heard something . . . a cry . . . or was it just the way the wind howled in the fireplace?

She had to get upstairs . . . had to find them. Suppose they weren't there? . . . Suppose she was too late? . . . Suppose it was like last time?—with those little faces so quiet, so distorted. . . . They had trusted her. Lisa had clung to her that last morning. "Daddy hurt me" was all she would say. Nancy was sure that Carl had spanked her for wetting the bed . . . had cursed herself for being too tired to wake up. She hadn't dared to criticize Carl . . . but when she made the bed, it wasn't wet; so Lisa hadn't wet the bed. She should have told them that at the trial, but she couldn't. She couldn't think, and she was too tired . . . and it didn't matter anymore.

The stairs . . . That was a post under her arm. . . . The stairs . . . three flights . . . Walk on the side . . . Be quiet. Nancy reached down and yanked off her sneakers. They were so wet they'd make a squishing noise. . . . *Important to be quiet. . . . Have to get upstairs. . . . Mustn't be too late again. . . . Last time too late. . . . Shouldn't have left children in car. . . . Should have known . . .*

The stairs squeaked under her foot. *Mustn't let him panic. . . . Last time he panicked. . . . Maybe Michael's call panicked him. . . . Last time they said the children hadn't been thrown in the water till after they were dead. . . . But Michael was still alive just a few minutes ago . . . Twenty minutes ago . . . and he thought Missy was sick. . . . Maybe she was sick. . . . Have to get to her. . . . The first flight. . . . Bedrooms on this floor . . . but no light, no sound. . . .* Upstairs two more flights. . . . On the third floor there was no sound either.

At the base of the last staircase, Nancy stopped to control her harsh breathing. The door at the head of the stairs was open. She could see a shadow against the wall caused by a thin flicker of light. Then she heard it . . . a voice—Michael's voice . . . "Don't do that! Don't do that!"

She ran up the stairs blindly, furiously. Michael! Missy! She hurried, not caring about the noise, but her thick socks didn't make noise. Her hand grasping the banister was silent. At the top of the stairs she hesitated. The light was coming from down the hall.

Silently, swiftly she hurried through the room, the living room probably, that was shadowy and quiet, toward the candlelight in the bedroom, toward the gross figure with its back to her that was holding a small struggling figure on the bed with one hand, giggling softly as with the other he pulled a shiny plastic bag over a blond head.

Nancy had an impression of startled blue eyes, of Michael's blond hair matting on his forehead, of the way the plastic clung to his eyelids and nostrils as she cried, "Let go of him, Carl! . . ." She didn't know she'd said "Carl" until she heard the name come from her lips.

The man spun around. Somewhere lurking in that gross mass of flesh, she could see eyes that darted and burned. Nancy had an impression of the plastic clinging, of Missy's tousled figure lying on the bed, her windbreaker a bright red heap beside her.

She saw the look of stupefaction replaced by cunning. "You." The voice was remembered. The voice that over seven years she'd tried to blot out. He started toward her menacingly. She had to get around him. Michael couldn't breathe.

He lunged for her. She pulled away, feeling his thick grasp on her wrist. They fell together, clumsily, heavily. She felt his elbow dig into her side. The pain was blinding, but his grip relaxed for an instant. His face was next to hers. Thick and white, the features bloated and broadened, but the sour, dank smell . . . the same as it had been before.

Blindly, she reached out with all her force and bit the thick, jowly cheek. With a howl of rage, he lashed out, but let her go, and she dragged herself up, feeling his hand pulling at her. She threw herself onto the bed, with her fingernails tearing at the tight plastic sheet that was making Michael's eyes bulge, his cheeks become blue. She heard his gasping breath as she twisted around to meet

Carl's new attack. His arms pulled her tight against him. She felt the sick warmth of his exposed body.

Oh, God. She pushed back his face with her hands and felt him bend her backward. As she tried to pull away, she could feel Missy's foot under her, touching her, moving. It was moving. Missy was alive. She knew it; she could feel it.

She began to scream—a steady, demanding call for help; and then Carl's hand covered her mouth and nostrils, and futilely she tried to bite the thick palm that was choking out air and causing great black curtains to close in front of her eyes.

She was sinking into gasping unconsciousness when abruptly the hands loosened their pressure. She choked—great gurgling sounds. From somewhere, someone was shouting her name. Ray! It was Ray! She tried to call out, but no sound came.

Struggling up onto one elbow, she shook her head. "Mommy, Mommy, he's taking Missy!" Michael's voice was urgent, his hand shaking her.

She managed to sit up as Carl swooped. His arm passed her and grabbed the small figure that had begun to squirm and cry.

"Put her down, Carl. Don't touch her." Her voice was a croak now, but he looked at her wildly and turned. Holding Missy against him, he ran away, his gait awkward. In the dark of the next room, she heard him bumping into furniture, and she staggered after him, trying to shake the dizziness. There were footsteps on the stairs now—hard, racing footsteps coming up. Desperately she listened for Carl, heard him down the hall; saw his dark shadow silhouetted against the window. He was climbing up the stairs to the attic. He was going up to the attic. She followed him, caught up with him, tried to grasp his leg. The attic was cavernous, musty-smelling, thick-beamed with a low ceiling. And dark. So dark it was hard to follow him.

"Help!" she screamed. "Help!" At last she could make her voice carry. "Up here. Ray. Up here!" She stumbled blindly after the sound of Carl's footsteps. But where was he? The ladder. He was climbing the thin, rickety ladder that led from the attic straight up to the roof. The widow's walk. He was going onto the widow's walk. She thought of the narrow, perilous balcony that circled the chimney between the turrets of the house.

"Carl, don't go up there. It's too dangerous. Carl, come back, come back!"

She could hear his harsh breathing, the high-pitched sound that was between sob and giggle. She tried to grab his foot as she climbed after him, but he kicked savagely when he felt her hand. The thick sole of his shoe caught the edge of her forehead, and she slipped down the ladder. Ignoring the warm, gushing blood that streamed down her face, not feeling the force of the blow, she started up again, crying, "Carl, give her to me. Carl, stop!"

But he was at the top of the ladder, pushing up the door that led onto the roof. Thick sleet pelted down as the door creaked upward. "Carl, you can't get away," she pleaded. "Carl, I'll help you. You're sick. I'll tell them you're sick."

The wind caught the door, pulled it open till it thudded against the side of the house. Missy was crying now—a loud, frightened wail: "Mommmmmmmy!"

Carl thrust his body onto the balcony. Nancy scrambled after him, bracing against the doorframe. It was so narrow. There was barely space for one person between the railing and the chimney.

Frantically she clawed at his clothes—trying to get a grip on him, to pull him back from the low railing. If he fell or dropped Missy . . . "Carl, stop. Stop!"

Sleet beat against him. He turned and tried to kick her again, but stumbled backward, grasping Missy against him. He lurched against the railing and regained his balance. His giggle was now a persistent, hiccuping sound.

The walk was covered with a layer of ice. He sat Missy on the railing, holding her with one hand. "Don't come any nearer, little girl," he said to Nancy. "I'll drop her if you do. Tell them they must let me go away. Tell them they must not touch me."

"Carl. I'll help you. Give her to me."

"You won't help. You'll want them to hurt me." He swung one foot over the rail.

"Carl. No. Don't do it. Carl, you hate water. You don't want water to cover your face. You know that. That's why I should have known you didn't commit suicide. You couldn't drown yourself. You know that, Carl." She made her voice calm, deliberate, soothing. She took one step toward the railing. Missy was reaching her arms out, pleading.

Then she heard it . . . a cracking, breaking sound. The railing was breaking! As she watched, the wooden posts gave way under Carl's weight. His head went backward; he swung his arms forward.

As he released his hold on Missy, Nancy darted forward and grabbed her baby. Her hands caught in Missy's long hair—caught and twisted and held. She was teetering on the edge of the walk; the rail was crumbling. She felt Carl grab her leg as he fell, screaming.

Then, as she was being dragged forward, firm arms came around her waist from behind—arms that held and supported her. A strong hand pulled Missy's head against her neck, pulled them both back, and she collapsed against Ray even as, with a last despairing scream, Carl slid off the balcony, across the icy, sloping roof and into the angry, rock-filled surf far below.

31

The fire licked hungrily at the thick logs. The warm hearth smell permeated the room and mingled with the scent of freshly made coffee. The Wigginses had opened the store and brought up cold cuts for sandwiches, and they and Dorothy had prepared a spread while Nancy and Ray were at the hospital with the children.

When they got home, Nancy insisted that the television crews and reporters be fed too, and Jonathan had thrown his home open to them. They had taken films of the homecoming of Nancy and Ray, carrying their children in from the car, and had been promised an interview the next day.

"In the meantime," Ray said into the microphones, "we want to thank everyone whose prayers through this day kept our children from harm."

The Keeneys had come back to the house too, wanting to be part of the gladness; frightened that they had waited to come forward with their information; sure that only prayer had made the rescue possible. *We are all so human, so foolish,* Ellen thought She shuddered thinking that her Neil had talked to that insane man. Suppose he had asked Neil to get into his car that day . . . ?

Nancy sat on the couch, tightly holding a peacefully sleeping Missy. Missy, smelling of Vicks and soothed with warm milk and aspirin, the ragged blanket she called her "bee" held securely to her face as she nestled against her mother.

Michael was talking to a gently questioning Lendon—telling all about it, thinking it out. His voice, at first excitable and rapid, was calmer now, even a little boastful: ". . . I didn't want to go away from that house without Missy when the nice man started fighting with the other man and yelled at me to get help. So I ran back up to Missy and called Mommy on the phone. But then the phone stopped working. And I tried to carry Missy down the stairs, but the bad man came. . . ."

Ray's arms were around him. "Good boy. You're quite a guy, Mike." Ray couldn't keep his eyes off Nancy and Missy. Nancy's face was discolored and bruised, but so serenely beautiful that he had trouble swallowing over the lump in his throat.

Chief Coffin put down his coffee cup and reviewed the statement that he would make to the press: "Professor Carl Harmon, alias Courtney Parrish, was pulled out of the water still alive. Before he died, he was able to make a statement, confessing his sole guilt in the murder of his children, Lisa and Peter, seven years ago. He also admitted that he was responsible for the death of Nancy Eldredge's mother. Realizing that she would have prevented his marriage to Nancy, he jammed the steering mechanism of her car while she was in the restaurant with Nancy. Mr. John Kragopoulos, whom Professor Harmon assaulted today, is on the serious list in Cape Cod Hospital with a concussion, but is expected to recover. The Eldredge children have been examined and were not sexually molested, although the boy, Michael, suffered a bruise on the side of the face from a violent slap."

The Chief felt fatigue settling into the very marrow of his bones. He'd give the statement and get home himself. Delia would be waiting for him, wanting to know everything about what had happened. This, he reflected, was the kind of day that made police work worthwhile. There was so much grief in this job. There were the times you had to tell parents that their child was dead. Moments like the one in The Lookout when they knew they had found both kids safe were to be cherished.

Tomorrow. Jed reflected that tomorrow he would have to judge his own culpability. This morning he had prejudged Nancy because of pique that he hadn't recognized her. By prejudging her, he hadn't let his mind stay open; had ignored what Jonathan and Ray and the doctor and Nancy herself were telling him.

But at least he had driven the car that got Ray to the balcony on the roof of The Lookout in that split second of time. No one else could have gotten up that hill on that ice so fast. When they'd seen Nancy's car crashed into the tree at the bend of the road, Ray had wanted to stop. But Jed had kept going. Some instinct made him feel that Nancy had gotten out of the car and was in the house. His hunch had been right. For that he could defend himself.

Dorothy quietly refilled Lendon's cup at his affirmative nod. Michael would be all right, Lendon thought. He'd come down and see them again soon. He'd talk to the children and to Nancy—try to help her to completely see the past for what it was and then turn her back on it. Nancy wouldn't need too much help. It was a miracle that she'd had the toughness to survive the horror of everything that had happened to her. But she was a strong person and would emerge from this last ordeal, able to look forward to a normal life.

There was peace in Lendon. He had compensated at last for his neglect. If he had gone to Nancy when Priscilla died, so much could have been avoided. He would have realized there was something wrong with Carl Harmon and somehow gotten her away from him. But then she wouldn't be here now with this young man who was her husband. These children would not be in her arms.

Lendon realized how much he wanted now to get home to Allison.

"Coffee?" Jonathan repeated Dorothy's question. "Yes, thank you. I don't usually have any this late, but I don't think many of us will have trouble sleeping tonight." He studied Dorothy closely. "How about you? You must be pretty tired."

He watched as an indefinable sadness crept over her face and understood the reason for it. "I think I must tell you," he said firmly, "that any kind of self-recrimination you have is intolerable. We all ignored facts today in a way that might have contributed to disaster. One of the first of these is that every single morning as I walked past this house, I have been annoyed by the glint that hit my eyes. This very morning I considered asking Ray to speak to the tenant at The Lookout about whatever he had in the window. With my legal training, I should have remembered that. An investigation would have led us to The Lookout very quickly.

"And one irrevocable fact is that if you had not elected to keep that appointment and bring Mr. Kragopoulos to that house, Carl Harmon would not have been deterred in his evil intent. He would not have had his attention distracted from Missy. Surely you've been listening to Michael's description of what was happening before your call."

Dorothy listened, considered, and in basic honesty agreed. A weight of guilt and remorse dissolved, and she felt suddenly light-hearted and glad, able to rejoice fully in the reunion. "Thank you, Jonathan," she said simply. "I did need to hear that."

Unconsciously, she clasped his arm. Consciously, he covered her hand with his own. "The roads are still treacherous," he said. "When you're ready to go home, I'd feel better if I drove you."

It is over, Nancy thought. *It is over.* Her arms tightened around her sleeping child. Missy stirred, murmured "Mommy," and slipped back into even, soft breathing.

Nancy looked at Michael. He was leaning back against Ray. Nancy watched as Ray gently pulled him down on his lap. "You're getting tired, fellow," Ray said. "I think maybe you kids had better get to bed. It's been quite a day."

Nancy remembered the feeling when those strong arms had grabbed her, held her, kept her and Missy from falling. It would always be like that with Ray. She would always be safe. And today she'd seen and known and been in time.

From the wellsprings of her being, prayer permeated her mind and heart: *Thank You, thank You, thank You. You have delivered us from evil.*

She realized that the sleet was no longer pelting the windows, that the moaning sound of the wind had died.

"Mommy," Michael said, and now his voice was sleepy. "We didn't even have a birthday party for you, and I didn't get you your present."

"Don't worry, Mike," Ray said. "We'll celebrate Mommy's birthday tomorrow, and I know just the presents to get for her." Miraculously, the strain and fatigue left his expression, and Nancy saw a twinkle begin in his eye. He looked directly at her. "I'll even tell you what they are, honey," he volunteered. "Art lessons from a really good teacher from the kids and a color job at the beauty parlor from me."

He stood up, eased Michael back into the chair and came over to her. Standing over her, he studied the part in her hair carefully. "I have a hunch you make a hell of a redhead, honey," he said.

Simon & Schuster
Proudly Presents

Where Are the Children Now?

BY Mary Higgins Clark & Alafair Burke

Available in hardcover and ebook at
SimonandSchuster.com
or wherever books are sold

Please turn the page for a preview of
Where Are the Children Now?

Prologue

She could feel the damp evening winds coming in through the cracks around the windowpanes. Only a few years earlier, an incoming draft in this room—her childhood bedroom—would have been unthinkable. Her mother had a discerning eye for detail that would have twitched at the slightest imperfection in a home, especially if it affected the comfort of someone sleeping under her roof. And her father had been the best Realtor on the Cape, the kind who had become an expert handyman over the years as an added service to his clients. But it wasn't only the seams around the windowsills that had cracked lately in the Eldredge family.

Eager to find sleep, Melissa stepped from the bed into her slippers and scuttled over to the window, not wanting to wake the rest of the house. After pulling the drapes closed, she located an extra blanket folded at the top of the closet, added it to the bed, and then entered a reminder in her cell phone to schedule an inspection of the entire house before she returned to New York, just in case she could ever convince her mother to sell it.

She was returning her phone to the nightstand when she got a new text message. *Are you still awake?*

She smiled to herself, appreciating the fact that Charlie had stayed in constant contact with her in the four days she had been here, the first time her brother, Michael, had been able to come back to the States since the funeral. *Barely*, she replied.

As much as Charlie traveled, he always checked in with her when he rose in the morning and before going to bed at night. *Any other ruffled feathers today?*

He was referring to the previous day's "silly sibling dust up," as her mother had called it dismissively. *All smiles and good behavior today. We visited the grave together.* The historic cemetery down the road from Our Lady of the Cape Church was the setting of the country-graveyard scene that hung over the piano in the living room, one of the numerous works of art that covered the home's mellow, creamy walls. When her mother painted that haunting row of headstones forty years earlier, the idea of someday burying her husband there must have seemed unimaginable.

She paused, recalling Michael holding first their mother's hand, and then hers, as they stood at the foot of their father's grave that afternoon. They were still family, no matter what. *Family is family,* she added. She never used to utter a negative word about them until she started grief counseling. Every time the subject matter of the Eldredges arose—and what had happened in their past—she found herself growing quiet, but she was told that talking about your childhood was an essential part of therapy. Nevertheless, she felt guilty sometimes, wondering if she spoke too frequently during counseling about the small hiccups in the family to the detriment of everything else. Today, at the grave, she had forgotten all about the occasional tensions and had been grateful once again for the wonderful life her parents had made possible for her.

She saw dots on the screen, indicating that Charlie was typing a new text. *Speaking of family, have I told you lately I can't wait for you to be my wife?*

He had proposed to Melissa two weeks ago, and she had immediately said yes. It had been her mother's idea for them to get married on the one-year anniversary of her father's passing, which was two months from now. The ceremony would be smaller than small—just the bride and groom, immediate family, and a few friends.

She found herself smiling as she typed a reply, as she always did when she thought about her future with him. *I was going to wait until tomorrow to tell you, but I passed the cutest little winery today. I know we said the courthouse, but maybe . . . ?* She hit send and then attached the photograph she had taken when they stopped on the way home from the cemetery to share a toast to her father.

Only seconds later, her phone rang in her hand. An incoming FaceTime call from Charlie. She accepted the invitation. "Well, hello there!" she chirped as his face appeared on the screen. He had close-cropped dark hair with clear blue eyes. And today, he sported a few days of facial hair across his square jaw.

"Too much texting," he said. "If we're talking wedding details, I at least want to see my fiancée."

"You got the pictures I sent of the winery?"

"I did, and it's absolutely perfect. That view is unbelievable!"

"But we already said we'd keep things simple and go to the courthouse."

"*You* were the one who was adamant about that."

Not long ago, Melissa believed that she would have a big, formal wedding with a reception at an iconic New York City venue—perhaps the Central Park Boathouse or the Rainbow Room overlooking Rockefeller Center. But when she had entertained those dreams, she imagined her father walking her down the aisle—and a man other than Charlie waiting for her at the altar. It didn't seem right to transfer her previous bridal fantasies onto a different relationship. Still, though, there might be something in between a fairytale wedding and the city courthouse. A small outdoor event at the winery felt like a good match for Charlie and her.

"But we already gave everyone the date. And told them it would be in the city."

He flashed that perfect smile of his. "*Everyone?* Everyone in this case is like . . . six people—all of whom adore you and would go to the moon if necessary to be there on your special day. *Our* special day."

At the mention of six guests, Melissa hoped that perhaps he was counting his sister, but Rachel Miller most definitely did not count as someone who "adored" Melissa. She had grudgingly agreed to meet Melissa, but only twice, and was reportedly furious when Charlie told her about his proposal, insisting that her brother was jumping into a new relationship too quickly. "Maybe Rachel will come around by then," Melissa said.

"Maybe so, or maybe not. We are getting married either way, and we are going to do it at this beautiful place you found for us. Consider it done. Let's book it."

"Really?"

"Promise. Text me the name of the place, and I'll call them first thing tomorrow for the details." And she knew immediately that the decision was, in fact, made. One of the thousands of things she adored about Charlie was the way he kept the trains running, always willing to take jobs off of her plate so she could move on to other tasks. "Oh, someone wants to say hi."

The camera on Charlie's phone shifted lower until she saw a chubby cheeked face gazing up toward her. Riley's fine blond hair was tousled in every direction in a look that could only be described as bedhead. Melissa could see cardboard boxes stacked on the kitchen floor behind her. They had just begun the process of slowly packing up his Upper West Side apartment since he and Riley would be moving in with Melissa.

"HI MISSA!" It sounded almost like *Missy*, her name until she suddenly announced in the first grade that she wanted to be called Melissa. Riley was smiling so hard, her eyes were nearly closed. "We miss you!" Behind the phone camera and out of view, Charlie told Riley to blow a kiss. Her pudgy hand found her pink heart-shaped lips and pressed. Pretty close for a not-quite-three-year-old.

"I miss you, too, sweetie. I'll be coming back to New York in two days."

Her future stepdaughter held her fingers up in a vee. "Two! Like me!"

"Except only two days, not two years."

"I know." She turned away from the camera and began toddling away.

"Tough crowd," Melissa said once Charlie returned to the screen.

"It's almost as if she has the attention span of a two-year-old," he said, shaking his head and chuckling. "Not to mention you're competing with the new Peppa Pig playhouse."

"How did she con you into letting her stay up this late?"

"She went to bed right after dinner but trotted out a while ago saying she heard noises. Figured I'd let her play while I finished up some work."

"Talk to you tomorrow?" Melissa asked.

"Always," he said. "And all the other tomorrows after that."

After they ended the FaceTime call, she forced herself to respond to three emails from a persistent attorney who didn't seem to understand the meaning of an out-of-office message before she finally turned off the nightstand light. When she closed her eyes, she pictured herself standing next to Charlie. She's wearing the white ankle-length silk halter dress she'd selected from Bloomingdale's last week for the occasion. He's wearing the tan linen suit she already told him would be perfect for a summer wedding, even at the courthouse. They're sharing the I-pronounce-you-husband-and-wife kiss under a teak pergola wrapped in sparkling white lights.

Riley runs toward them from the beach, roses braided in her hair, layers of pink tulle bouncing with every step.

She finds a swing set on the winery lawn and climbs into the seat, careful not to let her dress get caught in the chains. "Push me high!" Giggling and squealing, her nose wrinkling from her toothy grin. "Higher, Missa, higher!" She swings so high that she might fly right into the sky, where she'd blend in with the pink-white clouds. Her cries of joy subside as the swing's pace begins to slow. "Please Missa—don't stop pushing." But three more futile kicks and the swing is nearly still. As she turns her head to search for another boost, a sharp pinch seems to sting the back of little Riley's hand. She looks down toward the pain and sees a red mitten holding the chain of the swing, the image of a smiling kitten face sewn on the back. Why is she wearing mittens in summer? Her weight slumps forward before she can answer her own question, her body—so small, but suddenly so heavy—caught by someone. Someone.

In her dream, she wakes to the sound of a zipper. It's her own jacket being unzipped. Her nostrils are filled with the stench of baby powder and sweat. She feels the uncomfortable tug of her turtleneck being pulled clumsily over her neck, her undershirt moving with it. She stirs and starts to open her eyes. "Mommy, Mommy . . ."

When Melissa finally darted upright in her high school bed, she couldn't tell whether the scream she felt lingering in her throat and echoing in her ears was real or just another part of the nightmare. The house was silent except for the sound of the crash of ocean waves in the distance. Her neck was damp from perspiration, and, for just one second, she thought she detected the faint smell of talcum.

The girl on the swing wasn't Riley. It had been three-year-old Missy, and this was the most vivid dream yet. After forty years, after all of her efforts, all of her progress toward having a happy, future-focused life, Melissa was finally starting to remember. No, she prayed silently to herself. *Make it stop. I don't want to know. I don't want that to be me.*

Her fingers trembled as she pulled up Charlie's number. His voice was raspy when he answered. "Melissa? Are you alright?"

She hadn't thought to check the time. The bedside clock told her it was 2:30 in the morning. "It happened again. The dreams. They're getting worse."

1

Nancy came down the stairs, securing the back of the gold and pearl drop earrings she'd selected as the final touch to her ensemble. Her dress was a modest, but not matronly, silk shift. The bright royal blue was what Ray had always called her "signature color," bringing out the blue in her eyes. The subtle shimmer from the metallic embroidery around the neckline made it a bit more celebratory than her usual understated fare.

On the first floor, Melissa was sitting at the kitchen table in a fluffy white robe, sipping coffee, Velcro rollers the size of soda cans in her hair with a still-sleepy Riley on her lap. She put down her mug and sucked in an exaggerated gasp of approval. "Look at you! I don't know how I feel about this. The mother of the bride is not supposed to be the hottest woman in the room."

Nancy wrinkled her nose and shook her head. "Stop teasing me. And you shouldn't talk that way in front of this little angel anyway." Nancy leaned over and dropped a kiss on Riley's head, which she found warm and smelling of baby shampoo.

Riley gazed up at her with sleepy eyes and grinned. "She's right, Grand-Nan. You look really pretty." Nancy hoped that Riley's name for her—Grand-Nan—would never change.

She means you're hot, Melissa mouthed silently.

She noticed that Melissa was also looking especially beautiful today, and it wasn't only because of the full face of makeup she had already expertly applied. She was almost glowing with happiness. "You were able to sleep last night?" When she noticed how tired Melissa had seemed during her two most recent visits to the Cape, her daughter had explained she'd been having insomnia. Sometimes she worried that her ambitious little girl simply worked too hard for one person to handle.

"Like a baby. Thanks."

After all these years, Nancy was finally able to confine most of her thoughts to the here and now. Forty years ago, she would still lose herself in remembering. But she tried so hard to live each day in the present . . . not look back or try to predict the future. And eventually it worked, at least for the most part. She was seventy-two years old, and more than half of her lifetime had been as fortunate and blessed as any person could dare to hope for. When dark memories from the past did resurface, they tended to hit her either completely randomly, or—like today—at moments that paralleled her own life.

A *wedding*. Her daughter's wedding. A new son-in-law who adored Melissa, and an adorable little girl for Melissa to love and help raise. It was a time to celebrate. And yet . . .

The past never leaves. A *wedding*. Her mind fell not to Melissa's big day, nor even her own marriage to her beloved Ray, but to that other wedding day that altered her life forever. Nancy rarely felt like an elderly woman, and yet the fact that she had first married at the age of nineteen, as a college freshman, seemed nearly impossible now—not to mention the nightmare that followed. She had been determined to wear white for that wedding, so rushed after she lost her beloved mother. Nancy had owned only one white dress—a wool knit. It would do given the simplicity of their wedding plans, but then she saw the unexplained grease stain on the sleeve. If only she had connected the dots right then and there to her mother's car accident, there would have been no wedding to Carl Harmon and therefore no Peter and Lisa for her to mourn, even now, after all these years.

Her thoughts were broken by the sound of footsteps thundering down the stairs. She turned to see her son, Mike, in a perfectly tailored navy suit, his silk tie spotted with sailboats, looking proud of his sprint downstairs. "Like riding a bike!" he declared, holding up both arms like a gymnast who had stuck the perfect landing.

This house was an authentic old Cape with steps so steep they were nearly vertical. Ray used to say that the old settlers must have descended from mountain goats the way they built their staircases.

"Whoa, Mom, you look like a million bucks."

"You aren't too shabby yourself."

"You do look spiffy, Mike," Melissa chimed in. "But, really, you didn't need to splurge on a suit just for today. Weddings shouldn't be work for other people."

"I own a suit, little sis. Two of them, in fact. I'm a boat captain, not a cretin."

Forty years ago, Nancy had been so certain that she already knew her children to their core. Michael, always so organized, was the boy who not only followed instructions to the tee within seconds, but was the kid who told other children that they should fall in line as well. His baby sister, Missy, was the one who always managed to come home with a tear in her pants, bemoaning the loss of whichever beloved stuffed animal she had carried off on her latest pursuit of adventure.

In retrospect, Nancy could not believe how wrong she had been. Her rebellious little ragamuffin Missy was now Melissa, a star law student who became a prosecutor and was now a highly sought-after criminal defense attorney and outspoken advocate for criminal justice reform. Just the previous night, they had made a toast not only to the happy couple, but to the news that Melissa's true-crime podcast had hit the top 100 list on iTunes. Meanwhile, the previously earnest and somber Michael had lasted only three semesters in college before heading to the Caribbean for a "couple years off." Now he was a boat captain on St. Maarten, where everyone called him either Mike or Mikey.

Mike and Melissa even looked different. Mike was tanned and sinewy compared to his sister, with her alabaster skin and cherubic-like cheeks. While Mike's formerly blond hair became darker as he entered his tweens, Melissa still maintained the same strawberry blond curls she'd had as a child—the same as Nancy's hair until she relocated to the Cape and changed both her name and appearance. These days, Nancy was neither a redhead nor a brunette. Her perfectly groomed silver bob looked "regal," according to her hairdresser.

Mike pulled a phone from his front pant pocket and snapped a photo as Melissa held up a protective hand as if warding off the paparazzi.

"Nooo. I look ridiculous!"

"The last photo of you as a single lady. And the curlers are cute," he said, turning the screen so she could see the picture. "You should post this for your thousands of fawning social media followers. They'll love it."

Nancy braced herself for another round of sibling bickering. Would Melissa construe her brother's comment as backhanded criticism of her increasingly prominent public profile? Was that, in fact, Mike's intent? Nancy didn't want to take sides and wished they would just adore each other the way they had as children.

"You know what?" Melissa said, slipping Riley off of her lap. "I just might do that! Thanks. But first, I've got a dress I need to get into. Someone's getting married today!"

"You mean, you and Daddy," Riley added with a giggle. "I'm going to go find him now in the backyard if that's okay." She added an extra syllable to the word—not backyard, but *Bucky Ord* in the language they all affectionately called Riley-ese. Charlie had spent the previous two nights not literally in the backyard, but in the guest house so as not to see the bride right before the wedding. Ray and Nancy had built the addition to the property when Melissa was in college. They imagined they would need the extra room once the kids got married and began to have their own children. Now that was finally happening—at least for Melissa.

"Of course it's okay," Melissa said, giving her soon-to-be step-daughter a quick hug before pushing open the back door for her. "Let your dad know I'm counting down the minutes."

"I wish Mommy could be here," Riley said. "I miss her. She was too busy to come today."

Nancy could see her daughter's face briefly fall, the way it always did whenever Riley mentioned her mother. Riley was simply too young to understand the connection between her mother's death and the new role that Melissa now played in her life. She watched as Melissa placed a gentle hand on top of Riley's head. "I know, sweetie. We all wish she was here with you."

Once Riley slipped outside, Melissa explained. "Neil assures us it's completely normal for children to think they see their parents who have passed. It might even be in her dreams. It's a way to keep remembering them."

Neil Keeney was one of the neighborhood kids Mike and Melissa had stayed close friends with. He was also a talented psychologist working in New York City now. If he said there was nothing to worry about, Nancy believed him. Still, she knew how much Melissa wished she could take some of the child's pain away.

"Well, the person who *should* be here today for your husband is his sister," Nancy said pointedly. Melissa had reached out to Rachel personally, pleading with her to be here for her brother and niece, if not to bless their marriage.

Melissa waved a hand in the air as she walked toward the staircase. "Don't get me started on that one. I'm going to be around a very long time, and eventually she'll see the light. Charlie and I are determined not to let her decision ruin the day."

Nancy's eyes remained glued on Riley until she reached the sliding glass doors of the guest house. She suspected that as long as she lived, she would never be able to be in the presence of children without watching them as vigilantly as a member of the Secret Service. She smiled to herself as she watched Charlie, in the middle of knotting his tie, slide open the door to greet his daughter. He threw a wave in Nancy's direction before scooping up Riley to his hip. He was a good man—kind, understanding, loyal. Like her husband Ray.

As Melissa padded up the stairs and Mike flipped on ESPN in the living room, Nancy took a moment to breathe in the feeling of having her entire family—including two new additions—in this house. She could still remember the feeling of peace and welcome this place had given her when she'd first seen it, only in her mid-twenties, searching for a place to start over again. Ray had been the Realtor to help her find a rental. "The Cape is a good place to come when you want to be by yourself," he had said. "You can't be lonesome walking on the beach or watching the sunset or just out the window in the morning."

The moment Ray had brought her to this house, she knew that she would stay. The combination family and dining room had been fashioned from the old keeping room that had once been the heart of the house. She loved the rocking chair in front of the fireplace and the way the table was in front of the windows so that it was possible to eat and look down over the harbor and the bay. And then after they had married, he arranged for them to purchase the house, because he knew that she loved everything about it. It had now been a year to the day since she had woken up to find him cold beside her. Their physician said that Ray probably didn't feel a thing. His last words to her had been "I love you so much," as he'd crawled into bed with her on what they had no way of knowing would be their last night together. The memories they had made in this house belonged to both of them.

By the time she spoke aloud to her beloved home, there was no one else around to hear her. "Oh, how I'm going to miss you, old girl."

Be sure to check out the entire
UNDER SUSPICION SERIES
by Mary Higgins Clark & Alafair Burke

I'VE GOT YOU UNDER MY SKIN
9781476749082

THE CINDERELLA MURDER
9781476763699

ALL DRESSED IN WHITE
9781501108563

THE SLEEPING BEAUTY KILLER
9781501108594

EVERY BREATH YOU TAKE
9781501171734

YOU DON'T OWN ME
9781501171802

PIECE OF MY HEART
9781982132552

Available wherever books are sold or at
SimonandSchuster.com

Be sure to pick up a copy of these other bestselling thrillers by the
QUEEN OF SUSPENSE!

ALL BY MYSELF, ALONE
9781501131127

AS TIME GOES BY
9781501131097

MY GAL SUNDAY
9780671014919

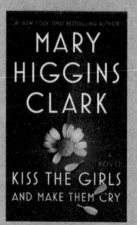

KISS THE GIRLS AND MAKE THEM CRY
9781501171772

Available wherever books are sold or at
SimonandSchuster.com

POCKET BOOKS
An Imprint of Simon & Schuster
A VIACOMCBS COMPANY